"Readers, beware! This book is a trap: once you start reading, you will not be able to stop. *Thirteens* is a deliciously creepy stay-up-all-night adventure that will shiver through you like a cold October wind. I loved every page!"
—**Jonathan Auxier**, *New York Times* bestselling author of *The Night Gardener* and *Sweep*

"Creepy, mysterious, and a whole lot of fun. *Thirteens* kept me up well past my bedtime. I can't wait to see what happens next!"
—**Cassie Beasley**, *New York Times* bestselling author of *Circus Mirandus*

"A sensational, spooky tale. *Thirteens* has all the creepy elements that I adore: a town with a wicked history, lovable characters, great writing, plenty of scares, and mystery layered upon mystery. Sign me up for the next book!"
—**J. A. White**, author of *Nightbooks*

OTHER BOOKS YOU MAY ENJOY

THIRTEENS

THIRTEENS

The Secrets of Eden Eld

BOOK 1

Kate Alice Marshall

VIKING

VIKING
An imprint of Penguin Random House LLC, New York

First published in the United States of America by Viking,
an imprint of Penguin Random House LLC, 2020
First paperback edition published 2021

Visit us online at penguinrandomhouse.com.

Library of Congress Cataloging-in-Publication Data is available.

Paperback ISBN 9780593117040

Printed in the United States of America

10 9 8 7 6 5 4 3 2 1

SKY

Design by Kate Renner
Text set in Perrywood MT Std

For my favorite palindrome.

One

Eleanor stared at the grandfather clock in the third-floor hall. It stood eight feet tall, made of dark oak. A bone-white pendulum hung within the case, carved like cords woven together in a loose diamond. It reminded her of the end of a key, but maybe that was only because of the keys that were painted on the wood around the clock face: thirteen identical keys in gold. The last key was almost entirely rubbed away.

The clock must be very old. It felt like it had tracked the passing of years and years. But she was not staring at the clock because it was tall, or impressive, or old. She was staring at for three reasons.

The first was that the clock hadn't been there when she went to sleep last night. Eleanor was sure of it. It stood opposite her door, and she felt certain she would have noticed an eight-foot-tall clock outside her bedroom or heard someone moving it into place.

The second was that those thirteen keys, gleaming against the dark wood, were the precise shape of the birthmark on her wrist.

The third was that the hands of the clock were running backward.

It's just a clock, she told herself. Nothing sinister. Maybe it had belonged to her grandparents, and Aunt Jenny had inherited it along with this house and the old car in the back shed that didn't run and the rambling, neglected orchard that spilled out behind the house like a half-grown forest.

Except that it hadn't been here last night.

And that wouldn't explain the keys. Or why the hands were moving backward—the second hand gliding from twelve to eleven to ten, all the way around to one; the minute hand clicking back every sixty seconds as the pendulum went left to right to left to right.

The clock chimed. The liquid, bottomless sound filled the hall, bouncing off the walls with their faded green wallpaper, spilling down toward the spiral staircase. Eleanor counted the chimes.

Seven.

Her phone agreed with the chimes—seven o'clock—but the contrary hands of the clock pointed instead to five and twelve. Seven hours backward from midnight, she thought, and rubbed the birthmark on her wrist reflexively.

"Eleanor!" Aunt Jenny called. "Come grab some breakfast

before the bus comes. You don't want to be hungry on your first day."

Eleanor didn't want to be *anything* on her first day of school at Eden Eld Academy. She didn't want to *have* a first day at Eden Eld Academy. But she had promised Aunt Jenny and Ben, and she had already broken enough promises.

She didn't want to turn her back on the clock, either, but she did, and scurried down the hall with her backpack over one shoulder. The boards creaked and groaned even with the hall rug to cushion her steps, and so did the stairs, which curled in a tight curve down to the first floor. She'd never lived in a house with a spiral staircase. Ashford House, which her grandparents had bought before her mother was born, had two of them. The house was full of odd things like that. Crooked hallways, skewed rooms, a stairway to nowhere. The clock ought to have fit right in.

Except—except she was sure, absolutely sure, it hadn't been there last night.

Aunt Jenny was in the kitchen, her back to the hall, pushing scrambled eggs out of a pan and onto an old china plate covered in a pattern of blue vines. Normally she had a thin face, like Eleanor, but right now it was soft and round, along with the rest of her. Her belly was so big she bumped against the counter, and as she finished with the eggs, she winced and muttered, "Oh, that's enough of that, you rascal," which meant the baby was kicking her ribs again.

Eleanor had always thought she looked more like Jenny than her own mother. They had the same brown hair, though instead of hanging straight down to her shoulders like Eleanor's, Jenny's sprang out around her face, escaping her braid. They had the same long nose, the same fair skin and murky green eyes, the same penchant for striped sweaters, and even the exact same glasses, but somehow Jenny always looked romantic and artistic, and Eleanor just felt gawky and plain.

Eleanor's step creaked a floorboard, and Jenny turned with a beaming smile. Too bright, Eleanor thought; it meant she was trying, which meant she wasn't *really* smiling. "Here you go, hon," Aunt Jenny said. The eggs steamed. The toast was perfectly toasted, just the right shade of brown. The jam was raspberry, thick and homemade.

Eleanor's stomach turned, and so did her mouth, downward in a little frown she couldn't stop. She pushed her glasses up, trying to use the movement to hide the frown.

"Nervous belly?" Aunt Jenny asked. She sighed, setting the plate down on the kitchen island between them. "I know it's tough. But if you don't start school now, you're going to get too far behind, and then you might have to stay back a year."

"I know," Eleanor said. She looked down at the Eden Eld Academy uniform she'd put on that morning—blue plaid skirt that fell to her knees, polo shirt, dark blue jacket with the school crest on the front. Everything was a bit too stiff and a touch too large. Aunt Jenny had worked hard to get her into Eden Eld instead of the public middle school, which was farther away and allegedly full of kids who cut school and watched R-rated movies without permission, which passed for juvenile delinquency in a town as sleepy as Eden Eld.

Eleanor was supposed to be grateful that she got into Eden Eld Academy, but it was hard to be grateful for anything these days.

"Couldn't you homeschool me, or something? I can learn on my own. It's all online now—I can design my own classes. You'd hardly have to do a thing."

Aunt Jenny put a hand on her belly and looked sad. Eleanor felt a twinge of anger that Aunt Jenny didn't deserve, but she couldn't help it. Every time someone looked at her like that, she felt like it was her job to cheer them up. To promise she was okay, even though she wasn't. Like *she* had to make *them* feel better, instead of the other way around.

"I would, hon. But with the baby due any day, and Ben working such long hours, we just can't. And Eden Eld is a great school. Your mom and I—" Aunt Jenny stopped. It was an unspoken rule that they didn't talk about Eleanor's mom. "Just give it a week or two, okay? And then we can see how it's going." She nudged the plate toward Eleanor. "Try some toast, at least?"

Eleanor bit back the urge to argue. Aunt Jenny was right. She had to go to school. Going to school was *normal*, and Eleanor needed to be normal. Needed everyone else to think she was normal. She'd made a plan. Her How to Be Normal plan.

1. *Don't talk about Mom.*
2. *Go to school.*
3. *Don't talk about things that aren't there.*
4. *Smile.*

So Eleanor smiled. She imagined puppet strings on the corners of her mouth, pulling them up. She made her eyes smile, too, wrinkling a little at the edges. That smile was the most useful kind of lie she'd learned to tell in the past couple of months. "Thanks, Aunt Jenny," she said, taking the toast. "I think I hear the bus. I'd better go."

She felt Aunt Jenny's so, so worried look on her back all the way to the hall.

She'd stepped out into the brisk late-October air before she realized she'd forgotten to ask about the clock.

But now she wasn't sure she should. The clock was strange. All of Ashford House was strange, but the clock seemed different. What if it was one of those things she saw that she shouldn't see? That wasn't really there?

Her mother saw things she shouldn't. Things she couldn't. Eleanor used to see them, too, but then she got better. But her mother hadn't. She didn't want anyone, especially Jenny, thinking she might be like her mom. Even if it was true.

Especially if it was true.

So Eleanor trudged up the driveway, determined to forget about the clock.

She hadn't really heard the bus. That was another lie. She

kept a list in the back of her mind of the lies she told Aunt Jenny and Uncle Ben. She'd pay off each lie, one by one, but for now she needed them. For now, the lies were what let her breathe and talk without coughing, without feeling smoke in her lungs.

She reached the end of the long dirt driveway and waited by the mailbox and the huge old pine tree that loomed there.

A chill wind sent a few dead leaves skittering and scuttering over the road, and the branches above her sighed and swayed. Mixed in with all those noises was another. Something rattling up in the tree: a clacking, hollow noise that sent a line of cold like a finger trailing down her spine. She craned her neck up, peering into the branches. They were drawn tightly together, the needles a prickly curtain hiding the trunk from her, but within them something moved. And the rattle came again. *Clackclackclack. Clackclackclack.*

Whatever was moving was big, and dark as the shadows around it. Eleanor's fingertips were cold, like she'd brushed them against ice. Her breath came out in quick puffs of mist, and she fought the urge to back away or run back to the house.

She was tired of being afraid. She'd had enough *afraid* to last her whole life. So instead of stepping back, she stepped forward, closer to the tree, and peered into those caught-together branches.

Clackclackclack. Clackclackclack.

The dark thing shifted and lurched. It looked like a crow, but much too big, made of ragged, overlapping shadows. She inched another step closer and then—then a big, yellow eye peered at her from between the branches.

She yelped, and now she did jump back, almost tripping over her own feet. She barely caught her balance and looked up quick into the tree again—but the eye was gone, and so was the shape, and so was the sound. She held her breath and she watched, but nothing moved. Only the wind making the branches shake.

The bus pulled up at the end of the drive. The doors hissed open. She still held her toast in one hand, hopelessly cold by now. She glanced back at the tree.

"Getting on?" the bus driver asked. She was a big woman, her body built in straight lines as if constructed entirely out of rectangles, except for her hair, which was frizzy and yellow and burst out in curls all around her face.

"Yes," Eleanor said. She couldn't see anything in the tree now. Nothing at all. She climbed on board. *Normal*, she reminded herself.

She didn't look back.

Two

Ashford House sat a couple miles out of what passed for downtown Eden Eld, far enough that the town border ran right through the middle of it, leaving the house half in and half out. Eleanor was the first one on the bus, and she took a seat all the way in the back, scrunching up in the corner. She watched the landscape flow by. Trees and more trees, mostly, and a few bare meadows, gone gray this late in the season. Not too many houses until they got closer to Eden Eld.

The bus stopped a few times, letting kids on one and two and three at a time, dressed in matching uniforms. Carefully pleated skirts for the girls, slacks for the boys, everyone wearing jackets bearing school crests, thirteen pine trees in a ring around a rose. They all ignored her. Good. She didn't want to talk to anyone. She didn't want to get to know anyone. She just wanted to get through the day and get home.

Not home. Back to Ashford House, because home was gone.

"Are you going to eat that?"

She jerked, startled, and realized that someone had taken the seat in front of her. He hung over the back, pointing at her toast with one hand while the other dangled loose. He had brown skin and glossy black hair that curled and tumbled and coiled every which way, hiding one eye. He looked like a pirate or a poet, or maybe a bit of both. He also looked hungry.

"I guess not," she said. "It's pretty cold."

He shrugged. "I don't mind."

She handed him the toast and he ate it in five massive bites before wiping his mouth with the back of his hand, then reached out to shake hers. She eyed the smear of crumbs and jam on his knuckles, then shook his hand anyway. She'd promised to be friendly. When her hand touched his, her skin prickled, like a bug running over her wrist. She shivered and pulled away. He looked a little puzzled, but his smile didn't falter.

"I'm Otto," he said. "Otto Ellis."

"Eleanor Barton."

"You're new."

"I knew that, actually," she said sharply. But he laughed, a bright, startling sound that made her grin on reflex, forgetting that strange, scuttling sensation in the face of his open friendliness.

"Sorry," he said. "I wasn't telling, I was just saying. I talk too much and point out the obvious. Or so I've been told."

"How could you tell? That I'm new?" she asked. Did she stand out? She'd planned on not standing out. It was basically her entire plan for surviving Eden Eld, in fact, and it was off to a bad start.

"It's a small school," he said. "Not that hard to memorize all the faces. Especially all seventeen of us that ride the number seven bus. Eighteen now, I guess."

He drummed his fingers on the back of the seat, then seemed to make a decision. He grabbed his backpack and swung himself around, plopping down in the seat right next to her and dumping his worn, dog-hair-covered backpack on top of his feet. She resisted the urge to scrunch farther away.

"Did you just move here?" he asked.

"Um. A couple weeks ago," Eleanor said. "But I was taking some time off."

"Was it because of your parents' jobs or something?"

"No," Eleanor said, flushing. Instinctively she pressed her fingertips against the flat, shiny skin on her palm. "It was—I'm staying with my aunt. At Ashford House."

His eyebrows went up, vanishing under the beautiful briar of his hair. "Ashford House? That weird, spooky place at the edge of town?"

"That's the one," Eleanor said, trying to sound as casual as she could. Ashford House made *normal* harder.

"Awesome," he said with feeling. "You know it's supposed to be haunted? Or some people say that, anyway, but I think it's just because it's big and old and weird. I went looking and it turns out no one's ever even died there, so how could it be haunted? And actually that's *really* weird given how old it is.

Somebody's died just about anywhere that's more than a hundred years old. Does it really have nine staircases?"

"Only seven," Eleanor corrected. He looked at her with rapt attention. She had to admit it was kind of nice, being the authority on something. "But they're really strange. There are two spiral staircases, and one that wraps around a corner at the very edge of the house and is so narrow Ben—that's my uncle—can't even get in. And one of them you can only get to if you walk through the giant fireplace in the living room, and it doesn't go anywhere at all. It just stops at a wall. And Uncle Ben says it's on the original plans that way, too. It never went anywhere."

"Cool," Otto said, grinning, and Eleanor couldn't help but smile back. "So why are you living with your aunt and uncle?"

Her smile wavered.

She could refuse to answer. Then she'd seem weird and rude.

She could tell him the truth. Then she'd seem weird and tragic.

Or she could lie.

"My parents died in a car accident," she said. Car accidents were normal.

He looked stricken. "I'm sorry. I shouldn't have asked."

"It's okay," she said, feeling guilty. But the truth would have only made him feel worse for asking. She added the lie to her list.

The bus pulled up in front of the school a few minutes later, and the rest of the students started grabbing their bags and rushing off. The school was a huge, imposing brick building, standing against the dark backdrop of the towering pines that were everywhere in Eden Eld.

One side of the front courtyard had been decorated with hay bales and scarecrows and pumpkins, and fake spiderwebs stretched over the front archway, but the Halloween decorations somehow made the place *less* spooky. It was scarier by itself, with its tall, narrow windows and the looming clock tower on the north side of the building.

Halloween. She'd been able to ignore that it was coming, holed up in Ashford House, but she couldn't get away from it now. Today was Wednesday. Saturday was Halloween, and that meant it was her birthday. She was going to be thirteen.

The first birthday she would celebrate without her mother.

"Who do you have first period?" Otto asked. She forced herself to look away from the decorations.

"Mr. Blackham?" she said. "Chemistry."

"Oh, he's great," he said. "He lets us light things on fire for science and make ice cream with liquid nitrogen, which is totally dangerous and awesome. I can show you how to get there, if you want. This place is kind of a labyrinth." He said *labyrinth* with clear enthusiasm for both the word and the concept. There wasn't any pity in his eyes at all. A little sympathy, but not that oh-you-poor-kitten look she was so used to. Her stomach balled up in one big knot. Now she felt even worse for lying to him. But how did you tell someone you just met *I live with my aunt because my mother tried to kill me?*

You didn't. Not if you wanted to be normal.

"That would be great," she said, feeling the puppet strings at the corners of her mouth. "That would be perfect."

THE DAY'S LESSON did not involve lighting anything on fire, for science or otherwise, to Eleanor's great relief. She knew fire too well now. She knew how different things smelled when they burned—walls, carpet, furniture. She knew the sound of glass cracking from heat and the grit of ash and soot that never seemed to scrub off her skin. So it was a relief to simply open a textbook and stare down at the diagram of a water molecule as Mr. Blackham directed them to the vocabulary lesson.

But they had hardly begun when a boy with mousy brown hair and mousy brown eyes darted in and handed a note to Mr. Blackham. He squinted at it before calling out, "Eleanor?"

She raised a tentative hand to shoulder height. He smiled a little, and she flushed. Of course he knew who she was. She was the New Girl. "Ms. Foster would like to speak to you," Mr. Blackham said. At her blank look, he sighed and pulled his glasses down his nose so he could look over them at her. "The headmistress. Left, down the hall, right, the office is right there."

"Is something wrong?" she asked. Her mind raced through every terrible thing she could imagine—Uncle Ben hurt at work. Something wrong with the baby, with Jenny. The house—houses as old as Ashford House had old wiring, too. All it took was a spark to start a fire.

"I wouldn't know," Mr. Blackham said, with the sort of tenderness that meant he knew about her mother and would be one of those adults who treated her like she was seven, not almost thirteen. "I'm sure everything's fine."

If he didn't know, he couldn't be sure.

She hopped off her stool and grabbed her bag. She hurried out of the classroom, a sour taste at the back of her throat. Her fingers found the shiny patch of skin on her palm. Without any students in the halls, her shoes echoed on the tiles, the sounds bouncing against the walls and falling back at her until it sounded like copies of her were walking to either side.

Being called to the headmistress's office wasn't good, was it? Not on her first day. Had she done something wrong? She couldn't think of anything. She'd been normal. Mostly.

Except for the clock, maybe. And the bird, maybe. But no one else knew about those.

Mr. Blackham's directions brought her to a large oak door, like something borrowed from a castle. She reached for the knob, but it flew open of its own accord, nearly hitting her. The girl who hurtled out of the office *did* hit her—a glancing blow on the shoulder that still nearly took them both tumbling to the ground. The girl caught her by the arm, hauling her upright.

At the touch, Eleanor's skin crawled, like insects scuttling over her wrist—the same feeling she'd gotten when Otto took her hand. The girl dropped her arm and blew out a breath, kicking loose strands of coppery hair away from her face. The rest of it was back in a sloppy ponytail. She wasn't wearing her school blazer, and her white polo shirt was wrinkled and only half tucked in to her slacks.

"Watch out!" the girl chided her. "Don't you know it's dangerous around here?"

"I—" Eleanor began, but the girl was taking off again down the hall already, her sneakers squeaking on the tile. Eleanor watched her go, rubbing her wrist, though the tingling had already stopped.

She shook her head. It was probably nothing. Nerves.

She turned back to the door, which had swung shut. Tentatively, she opened it. This time, nothing jumped out at her, and she stepped into the office. Inside, a gray-haired woman with purple lipstick sat typing at a computer. She looked up when Eleanor entered and pursed her lips.

"She's waiting for you," the woman said in the kind of scratchy voice you got from smoking cigarettes all your life, and pointed over her shoulder at a second, much less intimidating door leading to an interior office. Eleanor slinked past her desk. The woman started typing furiously.

The inner office door stood open a crack. Eleanor knocked tentatively, pushing it open a bit at the same time, and poked her head in.

A woman about her mom's age sat behind a huge oak desk that matched the large office door. The legs were carved into gnarled tree trunks that bulged outward before curving back in toward the wide, flat surface. The woman behind the desk had skin as milky as white marble, her features precise, giving her a sculpted look. She wore her orange-red hair scraped back in a tight bun. Her lipstick was bright red and her eyes bright green—everything about her was bright as polished gems. She made Eleanor think of serpents and of wicked queens, like in the fairy tales her mother used to read to her.

"Miss Barton. Please, take a seat." She waved at the armchair opposite her, across the desk, and Eleanor sank into it. She felt like she should say something, but she couldn't imagine what. Ms. Foster folded her hands on top of the desk and peered at her through black-rimmed glasses. "How is your first day going so far?" she asked.

"Um. All right," Eleanor said. "I was only in class for a few minutes."

"But you haven't encountered any problems?"

"No," Eleanor said. "No problems."

"Good. Very good. Now, I'm sorry that we haven't met before today. Normally I insist on meeting all of our students at some point in the application process—but you didn't have a normal application process, did you?"

"No, I guess not. I don't really know—I know my aunt—"

"Jenny is a delightful woman," Ms. Foster said with a wide smile. Her teeth were very white and very straight. "But it's not really on her account that I waived the usual procedure."

"It isn't?" Eleanor asked.

"Your mother. Claire. She was a dear friend of mine," Ms.

Foster said. "We grew up together, here in Eden Eld. When my father was the headmaster. We got into all sorts of trouble." She chuckled like she expected Eleanor to join in, but Eleanor's mouth was dry. No one had said her mother's name out loud to Eleanor, not that she could remember, since the fire. "I know that you are having a very difficult time right now. But I want you to know that you can come to me. For whatever you need," Ms. Foster said.

Her words overflowed with warmth, but a cold shiver went down Eleanor's spine. She mumbled that she understood. Her eyes dropped away from Ms. Foster's. It was hard to hold that bright green gaze.

A silver picture frame sat on the corner of Ms. Foster's desk. The photo was of a smiling Ms. Foster, in the same dark blue suit she wore now. Next to her stood a weary-looking man with gray at his temples and a long, sorrowful nose. And between them, their hands on her shoulders, was the redheaded girl who'd nearly knocked Eleanor over, a smudge of dirt on her cheek and a grin stretched so wide you knew she was faking for the camera.

"My daughter," Ms. Foster said. "Pip."

"We've met. Sort of," Eleanor said. If you could call that a meeting.

"My one and only," Ms. Foster said with a kind of sigh, and then she clapped her hands, making Eleanor jump in her seat. "Well! You had better get back to class. You don't want to get too far behind. So much to do and so *very* little time."

She smiled with those perfectly white, perfectly straight teeth. Eleanor stood. And then she paused. "You said you were friends with my mom?" she asked.

"Very good friends. Everyone knows each other in Eden Eld, of course, but Claire and I shared a number of interests in common," Ms. Foster said, tapping one long nail on the desktop thoughtfully.

"What kind of interests?" Eleanor asked.

"Oh, you know the sorts of things that teenage girls can get up to," Ms. Foster said. A strange look flashed over her face. Something that was nearly sadness, and nearly satisfaction. "Or you wouldn't know quite yet, I suppose. Claire and I had a special interest in local history. Though it led us to quite different places."

"I see," Eleanor said, though she didn't. She could tell that Ms. Foster wasn't going to say any more about it, though, and there was something very uncomfortable about standing in front of that huge desk with those perfectly green eyes fixed on her. She swallowed. "I should go, then."

"Wonderful," Ms. Foster said with another sparkling smile, and Eleanor backed away two steps before turning and hurrying from the room. She shut the door behind her and started to walk back out past the secretary's desk, but then she froze. The secretary had stopped typing and was staring in confused puzzlement at the last line she'd written.

Get out gET out GET OUT get OUT GeT OuT get oUt of Eden eLd

"Well," the secretary said in her hoarse, cigarette-wrecked voice. "Well." Her chin wagged back and forth, an odd sort of twitching, and she stabbed one yellow-stained finger against the backspace key. "Well. Well," she said with each stab, and one by one the letters vanished, until all that was left was a normal email. Then she blinked and smiled brightly at Eleanor. "Is there anything else you need, dear?" she asked.

"No," Eleanor said hastily. "Nothing, thanks."

She fled.

Three

Eleanor made it through chemistry without any more interruptions. Then she had math class (her second-weakest subject), and lunch (she looked for Otto, but didn't spot him), and then it was time for history, where they were informed by the energetic teacher, Ms. Edith Green, that they would be walking into town to conduct an educational scavenger hunt.

The rest of the class was pulling on their coats and chattering with the buzzy excitement of being let out of the stuffy classroom for the day when Pip Foster skidded into the room, every bit as disheveled as she had been that morning.

Ms. Edith—she insisted on being "Ms. Edith" rather than "Ms. Green"—sighed. "Late again, Pip," she lamented. "Punctuality is an important life skill." The corner of her mouth curled up in an odd little smile, one Eleanor would almost call *smug*. "Though I suppose it doesn't . . ."

She didn't finish that trailing sentence. Pip wasn't paying

attention, anyway. She'd spotted Eleanor and was staring at her openly, frowning. Eleanor's cheeks got hot. She looked away. And then she sneaked a quick sidelong look at the redheaded girl.

Eleanor hadn't liked Ms. Foster—hadn't liked the way she looked at Eleanor like she was a specimen in a jar, hadn't liked her too-sweet smile and the way she spoke to Eleanor as if she didn't really understand. The way you spoke to a pet. To be perfectly precise, she gave Eleanor the creeps. And when Pip had touched her, she'd gotten that crawling feeling over her skin. But then, it had happened with Otto, too. And she liked Otto.

So what did that mean about Pip? Pip seemed nothing like her mother—like she'd gotten her looks and nothing else. Every inch of Ms. Foster was polished and controlled, while Pip seemed like she had so much energy that it knocked everything a little askew, from her mussed hair to her untied shoelaces. She'd doodled in purple pen on her arm, squiggles and stars and exclamation points, and there was a birthmark peeking out of the collar of her shirt, where her neck and her shoulder met.

Was that a key?

Eleanor blinked, looking more closely, but Pip had shifted her bag on her shoulder, and the birthmark—if that was what it was—disappeared.

"It's rude to stare," Pip told her, but half her mouth hooked up in a grin. Then she darted out of the classroom after the rest of the students, leaving Eleanor to trail behind.

She'd probably just imagined the birthmark. And she'd probably imagined the thing in the tree, and the wickedness in Ms. Foster's smile. This place was normal. She was normal.

Everything was going to be fine.

IT WAS A short walk from the Academy to the town square. If it weren't for the modern cars, it would have been like walking through a time warp. Eden Eld was all cobbled streets and stately pines, quaint little buildings with bright white shutters, and, even this late in the season, tidy little beds of flowers everywhere. Even the autumn leaves had fallen in an orderly fashion, the perfect shades of red and yellow and orange, not one of them turned brown and lumpy.

The few flowers that were still in bloom peeked out from window boxes and along the edges of walkways. They were all the same kind, one that Eleanor had never seen before she came to Eden Eld. They had reddish purple petals that were oddly thick, and their leaves were long, with jagged edges. They were beautiful, Eleanor supposed, but unsettling, too. Those leaves looked like they might prick you. But something about them was familiar.

"Gather up!" Ms. Edith called, waving them toward her in the center of the town square. It was a tidy little plaza with trees—ringed by the flowers—on each corner and a monument at the center, a stone pillar with words carved on its imposing granite surface. "Take a worksheet, find a partner, and fill in the answers as you find them. You are free to wander, but be back in thirty minutes to turn in your papers. And if you're not sure where to search, ask around! Learning is *connection*! History lives in all of us!"

Ms. Edith's eyes were feverishly bright with the power of learning. Off to Eleanor's right, Pip snorted and rolled her eyes a little. Eleanor hid a smile. Ms. Edith *was* a little overenthusiastic. She was younger than Aunt Jenny, and Eleanor was guessing she hadn't been teaching long.

But she was thinking less about Ms. Edith and more about the assignment. Letting them wander? Talk to the locals? It would have been unimaginable at her old school. But she'd heard it over and over again: *Eden Eld is the safest town west of the Mississippi.* Why the Mississippi, she always wondered.

But they were right. She'd looked it up. Eden Eld's crime rate was effectively zero. They only had one police officer, and she mostly directed traffic. *The perfect place to raise a family,* their website said. *Our children are our future.*

"Do you want to buddy up?" Pip asked her, shuffling over with a look of bored resignation. She gestured vaguely with the pair of worksheets already in her hand. "I've done a million of these things. We can probably knock it out in five minutes and go get some cocoa or something."

"I, uh—"

"Otto said to look out for you," Pip said, like this explained something. "He said you're all right." She seemed unconvinced, but open to the possibilities.

"You know Otto?" Eleanor asked.

"Everyone knows everyone here," Pip said. "It's the worst. Except Otto, obviously. He's the best. Even if he is a giant dork. So what do you say?"

Eleanor bit her lip. She wanted to be friends with Pip, in a way that also made her want to hide in a very deep hole or a very dark closet and hope that Pip never looked at her again because what if she did something *weird* and Pip told Otto and then neither one of them ever spoke to Eleanor ever again and she had to change her name and move to Poughkeepsie and—

"Great!" Pip declared, as if Eleanor had answered her, and shoved the second worksheet into her hands.

"Oh. Okay. Thanks," Eleanor managed. She took the offered worksheet and looked at the first question. "'*What is written on the Founders' Monument?*'"

"I already got that one," Pip said. "I can fill it in for you." She reached for the paper.

"Philippa, the *spirit* of the assignment is as important as the *letter* of the assignment," Ms. Edith said, drifting by on a cloud of instructional bliss.

Pip sighed. "I liked her better when she was my babysitter. At least then I didn't get graded," she confided. She jerked her chin toward the granite pillar, which several students were clustered around. Eleanor hadn't had a chance to learn people's names yet, which made her feel as if there were a barrier between her and the rest of them, like a foggy pane of glass she was stuck on the wrong side of.

She hadn't felt that with Otto. And strangely not with Pip either, who shouldered her way through the small crowd. Eleanor clung close, taking advantage of the gap behind her. Pip reached the monument and flourished her hands. "Ta-da," she said, and then, conspicuously looking away, recited the words on the monument. "*In honor of those present at the signing, for ensuring the safety and prosperity of Eden Eld for generations to come.*" She continued with the three short lines inscribed in blockier text beneath. "*Eden Eld. Founded 1851. Drawn Onward.*' Kind of a terrible town motto, if you ask me, but weirdly they didn't."

Eleanor dutifully scribbled the answer—the space provided wasn't big enough, and she had to turn the page and write in the margin, too. "What about the numbers?"

"What numbers?" Pip asked, looking at her.

Eleanor pointed. Halfway between the text and the ground was a tiny set of numbers carved carefully into the stone, each one no more than half an inch tall. *31313.*

"Huh," Pip said. "I never noticed those before." She gave Eleanor a suspicious look, like maybe she'd stealthily carved them there herself. But then she just shrugged and added the numbers to her answer.

The rest of the students had wandered off, having finished with the first task, and were spreading out as they tracked down other entries on the worksheet. Pip skimmed the sheet and gave a decisive nod.

"'A founder's hands made these hands. What date is on my base?' That means the clock tower—hands, get it? Bartimaeus Ashford built it. There's a plaque on the side with the date it was built. And it is *right* next to Betty's Bakery, which has *the* very best cocoa. We'll do that one next."

She grabbed Eleanor's hand to pull her along. The instant their hands touched, that feeling shot through her again— except this time it was less like a bug crawling on her skin and more like a *zing*, a tingle that ran all the way from the bones of her hand to the socket of her shoulder. Pip looked down at their hands and then at Eleanor with a frown.

Had she felt it, too? But then she was off again, tugging Eleanor behind her, moving at a half run like it was the slowest setting she had. She leaped over a hay bale, and Eleanor was forced to follow, narrowly missing putting her foot down on the lumpy brow of a grinning pumpkin. Cheerful ghouls and glittering ghosts laughed from every window. It seemed like all the decorations were smiling. Smiling scarecrows, smiling spiders, smiling werewolves in overalls and straw hats. She'd never seen such a *happy* Halloween. It was a bit unsettling. And everywhere, the purple flowers grew, their petals peeling back from their centers like sneering lips.

"'And even in the autumn and through the coldest winters the flowers bloomed,'" Eleanor whispered. Pip slowed down a bit, bringing the pace to a brisk walk, and looked back. She'd let go of Eleanor's hand, but Eleanor still felt tugged along behind her.

"What was that from?" Pip asked.

"A fairy tale," Eleanor said. That's what the flowers reminded her of—her mother's book of fairy tales. *Thirteen Tales of the Gray*, it was called. She'd read it to Eleanor every night when she was little.

A pang went through her, soft sorrow wrapped around sharp anger and neither of them right. The book had burned, with everything else in the house.

"Well, it's true," Pip said. "They bloom all year round, every year. And Eden Eld is the only place they grow." She nudged one of the flowers, which was growing in the strip beside the sidewalk. Its head bobbed, and the gathered petals smacked against the toe of her shoe, the movement like a striking snake.

They'd reached Betty's Bakery, Eleanor realized, a small, quaint building with the three-story clock tower looming behind it; that was why Pip had stopped. The smell of cinnamon and chocolate wafted out. A deep window seat at the front was filled with a Halloween display of intricately carved pumpkins. One read *Betty's Bakery* in spooky script. The others showed a hissing cat, a wolf howling at the moon, and a bird with a wicked-looking eye. A man sat at a table out front, whistling as he carved a new one, a bucket of pumpkin guts beside him and newspaper covering the table.

"The clock tower's right around the corner," Pip said, somewhat unnecessarily. "If you go fill out the worksheets, I can get us cocoa. We can drink while we go find the other stuff."

"Okay, yeah, you got it," Eleanor said quickly and loudly,

sounding like a complete weirdo, she was sure. She felt her ears go hot. She was, it turned out, really pretty terrible at being normal. But Pip didn't seem to mind.

A wide, cobbled courtyard stretched between the bakery and the building next door, and exactly in the middle stood the steep stone walls of the four-sided clock tower. It was *just* a tower, with no building attached to it or anything, the base maybe ten feet by ten feet across. A wrought-iron gate blocked off the back of the courtyard. On the other side stretched an empty lot and then the tall, imposing shapes of the pines.

Eleanor hadn't thought the trees were that close to town. From among the buildings, everything was so open and bright. Yet there the forest waited, just out of sight.

She crossed the courtyard to the mural of the clock tower. The side nearest her didn't have anything on it. She walked all the way around the back and to the other side before she found the brass plaque that told the story of Bartimaeus Ashford, the youngest of the founders, who was an architect and clockmaker. The same Ashford who had built Ashford House, of course, and a bunch of other buildings in town. And the tower seemed just as strange as the house, in its own way. Ashford House had too many doors and stairs; the tower didn't seem to have any. Wouldn't it need to be repaired? Wound? Cleaned, even? But there were no doors on any of the four sides.

Weird. She shook her head and reminded herself that she wasn't just sightseeing: she had to fill out the worksheet.

Pip had said that the date on the plaque was the date the

clock tower was built, but she must have remembered wrong. The only date was Bartimaeus's birthday: September 28, 1842. *The date of Bartimaeus Ashford's death is unknown,* the plaque added. That, Eleanor thought, was odd as well. If he was so famous, shouldn't they know when he'd died?

The skin on the inside of her wrist prickled, and she glanced to her right, not quite knowing why. She froze.

There, in the empty lot, stood a giant black dog. It panted, huge clouds of mist rolling out over its red tongue. Its eyes were red, too, and stared straight at her. It took a step toward her, its head dropping, its tail stiff and straight out behind it.

"I got you extra whipped cream," Pip said loudly, coming around the corner. Eleanor's eyes stayed locked on the dog. It growled, the sound vibrating through the air until it rattled her teeth in their sockets. "Here you go. Eleanor? Earth to Eleanor, we've got cocoa, come in, Eleanor."

"Don't you see the—" Eleanor started. Pip couldn't have missed the dog. It was standing right there. But it was like she didn't see it at all. Which meant . . . which meant Eleanor was definitely seeing things that weren't there.

It had started again.

She forced herself to turn away from the dog. She smiled. "What do I owe you?" she asked.

"Nothing. My mom gives me a ton of allowance to make up for the fact that she has the maternal instincts of a sea slug," Pip said, and handed over the cocoa. "Shall we go discover what kind of tree adorns the sign in front of the library?"

Don't turn around. Don't look at things that aren't there.

"Let's go," she said with feeling. Pip grabbed her hand again and led her back around the front of the building, moving with enough speed that Eleanor had to be careful not to spill her cocoa. She listened for a growl, or the rattle of huge paws hitting an iron gate, but nothing came.

And then they were out of the alley and back in front of the bakery, where the man carving the pumpkin sat with a puzzled look on his face, scratching his chin and staring at what he'd made. He'd carved the pumpkin with words, and around them were ragged marks, like he'd plunged his knife into the pumpkin again and again without any artistry. Thirteen ragged marks, and two words.

GET OUT.

As they walked down the street, she almost thought she heard him crying.

Four

Back at the town square, Ms. Edith collected their work-sheets and, with a skeptical look at the empty cups of cocoa, declared Pip and Eleanor the winners, being the only ones with completely correct answers. As they walked back toward school, Eleanor kept glancing side to side, expecting to see that huge black dog again, and hoping desperately that she wouldn't—or that someone else *would*, and prove that she wasn't seeing things that didn't exist.

It wasn't the first time that Eleanor had seen something no one else could. No one else had seen the man at the bus stop back home, either. Or the others that she'd learned not to talk about. That she had, eventually, stopped seeing.

They reached the classroom just as the period ended, and the students dispersed to their next classes. Pip hesitated at the door. "Eleanor," she said, and let the word hang. Then she shook her head. "Never mind. It was nice to meet you. We can hang out again tomorrow, if you want."

"I'd like that," Eleanor said. She was surprised to find the smile she gave Pip was entirely genuine.

"I have to get to gym class," Pip said. "Be careful, okay?"

"What do you mean?" Eleanor asked, startled, but Pip only shrugged and dashed away, leaving Eleanor staring after her.

ELEANOR DIDN'T SEE Otto on the bus home, and she rode alone in the back, pulling her feet up on the seat. She'd had exactly one goal today: get through it with everyone thinking she was normal. And could she really say she'd failed? She hadn't done anything weird. Weird things had happened around her, but that didn't count, did it?

Except that she was the only one that had noticed. Which meant it *was* happening again. Just like it had before, when she was little. Just like it had right before her mother set the fire that burned down their house and nearly killed Eleanor.

She felt wobbly, almost dizzy, her thoughts fuzzy the way you got when you didn't have enough water and stayed outside all day in the sun. She'd expected that coming to Eden Eld meant leaving this kind of thing behind her.

Eleanor still wasn't sure what *this kind of thing* was, except that it made her smell smoke again, and feel ash clinging to her skin. It made her start coughing, until the bus driver glanced up at the rearview mirror to look at her.

She'd been lucky to get out. When she'd seen the stairway all up in flames, she'd covered her mouth and dropped to the floor and crawled to the bathroom, which overlooked the garage. She'd climbed onto the garage roof and scrambled down the gutter, and then she'd run back to the front door to try to get in, because her mom was still in there.

She still had a shiny burn scar like a crescent on her right palm, where she'd touched the doorknob. The fire had been so hot it heated the knob all the way through. She couldn't get in. She couldn't help.

But it turned out her mother *wasn't* still in there. They'd searched all over after the fire was out, and there was no body. But the police were sure, completely sure, that a person had set the fire—right at the bottom of the stairs. They told her that her mother had set the fire, and then she'd just . . . left.

Whenever Eleanor thought about it, she felt like she was touching the doorknob again—feeling that bite of pain, with so much more waiting on the other side. It filled her with so much rage and so much sorrow that all she could do was keep the door closed and try to feel nothing at all.

The police had looked for her, of course, and asked Eleanor all sorts of questions. About the strange things her mother said, about what they called her *erratic behavior.* They had called in a psychologist to talk to her, and he explained it like she was six. That her mother was *sick in her brain,* and she'd said, *You mean she's mentally ill,* and the man had blinked three times behind his big glasses and said, slowly, *Well. Yes.*

And then she'd done the one thing her mother had told her not to do all her life.

She went to Eden Eld, to live with Aunt Jenny.

The bus pulled up in front of Ashford House. She walked down the steps, coughing into her elbow one more time. The branches of the tree in front of the house shook, and something scraped along the wood. Eleanor walked quickly to the front door, not breaking her stride until it was shut firmly behind her.

When she was little, before she realized that the things she saw, that her mother saw, weren't real, her mother would put her arms around her in bed and whisper to her.

There are things in the world that shouldn't be, she would say. *Things out of place. Little pieces of other worlds that slipped in, like a piece of gravel in your shoe. Some of them are kind, but most of them are dangerous. Be careful, Elle, and stay away from Eden Eld.*

She'd always wanted to protect Eleanor. So Eleanor couldn't understand why she would have set the fire. Everyone seemed so sure—but they were sure that the things her mother was afraid of weren't real, and Eleanor knew better. Her mother *was* ill—her fear crawled inside her and grew and grew until she couldn't breathe or think straight. She was ill, *and* the things she saw were real.

Eleanor had thought the fact that she stopped seeing them meant that she was safe, and that her mother's growing panic was only a symptom of her illness. But now they were back. Eleanor knew it didn't mean her mother hadn't been sick.

But it *did* mean that she'd been right.

And maybe it meant there was more to the fire than everyone thought.

BEN DIDN'T MAKE it home for dinner, and she and Jenny ate in front of the TV, Jenny with her plate balanced on her huge belly. They watched a show about a group of good-guy thieves, and at the end of the episode all the bad guys were ruined and all the good guys were happy, and Eleanor lost herself in a world where all wrongs could be righted in forty-three minutes (plus commercial breaks). By the time they were done, Jenny was yawning, and she headed off to bed with a "night, Elle," leaving Eleanor on her own.

It had started raining outside, drumming pleasantly against the roof and the windows. She'd always liked the sound of rain, as long as she didn't have to get wet. She pulled her sweater tight around her as she made her way to her room and pushed open the door.

She was surprised to see something waiting on her bed. A book. She didn't remember leaving a book there. The one she'd been reading was on the bedside table, in fact.

She crossed the room, frowning. And then she stopped

dead, her thoughts turning into a wild tangle that made no sense at all.

It was her mother's book. *Thirteen Tales of the Gray.*

It must be another copy. Jenny had left it here, or—but no. It was the same book. The *exact* same book, the same wear on the spine, the same streak of pink, glittery paint from a close encounter with one of Eleanor's early craft projects. It should have burned, but the only evidence of the fire was a few smudgy spots of ash.

She sat on the edge of the bed and pulled it toward her. The rain had stopped. The house was silent. "You can't be here," she said. The book, unconvinced, remained stubbornly real.

In the hall, the clock chimed the hour.

Five

Eleanor slept with the book beside her on the bed. She had odd dreams of something soft and almost uncomfortably warm on her chest, pinning her down, and she woke drenched in sweat and smelling faintly of ash. There were little smudges of it on her covers, too, and on her clothes. They must have come from the book. And the book . . .

She didn't know if she wanted to think about where the book had come from.

She was afraid that Otto wouldn't be on the bus again, but he came bounding on when they reached his stop, looking more rumpled than he had the day before. "Sorry I missed you yesterday," he said immediately. "I went over to help my dad at the clinic. A border collie was giving birth. There were nine puppies. *Nine.* How would you like to have nine babies all at once?"

"One seems like more trouble than I'm interested in," Eleanor confessed. "My aunt's pregnant," she clarified.

"Oh, neat. I love little kids," Otto said. "I've got three little sisters—triplets—so liking them might just be a survival strategy. The only thing I like better than little kids is probably animals. All animals. Dogs, cats, horses, lizards . . ."

She wondered if, given the chance, he would name every type of animal in the ecosystem. But the bus went over a sharp bump, and it seemed to derail his train of thought. For the rest of the ride, Otto talked about the veterinary clinic his dad ran, his dog, his sisters, the relative size of the planets in the solar system, and the Yellowstone supervolcano. Eleanor listened, happy to let someone else fill the silence. Eden Eld Academy used a block schedule, which meant Eleanor had a whole new set of classrooms to find today. Luckily, her first class of the day—English with Ms. West—she shared with Otto.

"Pip's in it, too," Otto said. "You met Pip yesterday."

"Yeah, I know," Eleanor said, laughing.

"Right. Of course you do. My mom says I need to install a better filter between my brain and my mouth."

"I don't mind," Eleanor said, shaking her head, and followed him through the echoey school hallways. The fairy tale book was in the bottom of her bag, and it seemed to make it heavier as she walked. She hadn't opened it yet, but she didn't feel comfortable leaving it at home. She didn't understand how it had gotten into her room.

Had her mother left it for her?

But that was impossible. Her mother was gone. She'd run off—abandoned Eleanor and worse. Eleanor hated her. *Hated* her, and so hated the book, too. Except she also loved her mother and so she kept the book, kept it close, and wished she knew what she was supposed to do and what she was supposed to feel.

Otto led her to a corner table when they arrived, which was already occupied by two other students. The other two kids, a girl and a boy, sat so close together they kept bumping shoulders, and they were whispering about some show they had watched the night before.

Ms. West spotted Eleanor and smiled, then walked over with a textbook and a tidy stack of papers.

"Eleanor, isn't it?" she asked. "Welcome to Eden Eld Academy. I'm Ms. West. Obviously!" She chuckled, like this was a grand joke. She had skin that reminded Eleanor of dough that had just finished rising. Soft and somehow vulnerable. She set the textbook and the papers in front of Eleanor and tapped them twice with nails painted the color of overripe blueberries. "Here's everything you need for now. I've already checked out the textbook under your name, and this is right where I was going to put you." Her eyes strayed to the empty seat on Otto's right, but just then the door burst open and Pip skidded into the room, her cheeks bright red from exertion.

"I'm here! The bell hasn't rung!" she said, just as it did.

Ms. West laughed. "Just in the nick of time, Pip! Well, now that we're all here . . ."

Ms. West made her way up to the front of the class, already rambling about the plans for the week.

Pip scurried to the empty seat next to Otto and fell into it with a gusty sigh.

"You literally live on school grounds, Pip," Otto said, eyes twinkling. "How are you *always* late?"

"My mom was on the phone with *subject three*," she whispered. "I was trying to listen in. I got this dish thing in my spy kit that lets you listen to conversations from far away, and I was testing it out."

"And?"

"Nothing interesting," she said. "Just 'How are things going? Oh, very good here, too. Everything should be set for the big event.' And then goodbyes."

"It's probably just some January Society thing," Otto said.

"Obviously it's a January Society thing. An *evil* January Society thing." Pip's voice barely rose above a whisper, and Eleanor got the feeling she wasn't supposed to be listening—but she couldn't help it.

Otto rolled his eyes. "They are not evil. They do bake sales. Evil cults don't hold bake sales."

"Apparently they do," Pip said.

Eleanor couldn't tell if she was joking. She had been trying not to stare too hard while they talked, but Pip fixed a hard look on her.

"Are your parents in the January Society?" Pip asked.

"No," Eleanor said at the same time as Otto. He blushed a bit.

"Eleanor just moved here," Otto said. "Remember?"

"I know. But she's a Barton. So your family's from here, aren't they?" Pip asked.

"Shemovedheretolivewithheraunt," Otto said, very fast and rather loudly. "At Ashford House."

"And I don't think Ben and Jenny are part of any societies. They donate to the ACLU?" Eleanor supplied, uncertain if this counted.

Pip lit up. "Wait, do you really live at Ashford House? That's awesome. You should have told me that yesterday, Otto! Jeez."

"Pip! Please keep cross talk to a minimum," Ms. West said. Pip's ears turned scarlet at the tips, and she started quietly scribbling in the margin of her class notebook, twisting lines with jagged bits like thorns.

Eleanor glanced out the window as Ms. West handed out study packets. It looked out over an empty meadow beside the school, more of a random break in the looming pines than anything intentional. The grass grew a good foot high, and a low morning mist clung near it, giving everything a hazy, spooky look.

In the middle of the field stood the black dog. Steam spilled between its fangs. A gob of saliva dripped from one side of its jowls, and though she couldn't hear it, she was sure it was growling.

Ms. West had reached her. She followed Eleanor's gaze and smiled. "It's such a lovely campus, isn't it?" she asked. She set her hand on the back of Eleanor's chair and sighed. "Positively picturesque. Oh, that I were a poet, and could describe it as it deserves. But that's what I have all my budding young Wildes and Byrons and Shakespeares for!" She clapped Eleanor on the shoulder and wandered away again.

Otto bumped Eleanor's hand with the very tip of his smallest finger. He looked down at his paper as he whispered. "Don't stare at it," he said. "You don't want them to know you can see."

Eleanor's fingertips felt cold again, ice creeping up toward her knuckles.

He'd seen it.

She wanted to ask him what he saw, but he had his head down, reading the story in the copied pages. Pip had the exact same pose, shoulders bowed, head down, but her eyes were lifted to Eleanor. Her look was intense and serious. She saw it, too.

She'd seen it yesterday. She'd pretended not to, but she *must* have. Why hadn't she said anything? Surely she knew that Eleanor could see the dog, so why let her think that she was the only one?

Why let her think she was alone?

Eleanor chanced one last look out the window. The dog was gone.

LOOK OUT OF *the corner of your eye,* her mother had said to her, sometime in those last few horrible days. *Don't look straight on. Always look at them sideways. That's how to keep yourself safe.*

She'd never told anyone. Certainly not now. They'd think she was like her mother. They'd think she was sick and needed help. Maybe she was.

But Otto and Pip had seen it, too. *That* had never happened before.

Lunch was quinoa and a fall vegetable curry made from locally harvested vegetables (ALL WITHIN THIRTY MILES! said the placard in the lunch line). At Eleanor's old school, Thursdays were usually sad, flat hamburgers that didn't even have any toppings. She wished she were hungry enough to enjoy the change.

Otto and Pip found Eleanor in the lunch line. As soon as she had her food, they dragged her off to the edge of the front courtyard near the hay bales. There was a little wooden sign next to the decorations that read DONATED BY THE JANUARY SOCIETY. Pip kicked it over with her toe as she sat down.

"So," Pip said, as soon as they were all sitting. "You saw it. The dog." Her voice was hushed.

"The one with glowing red eyes?" Eleanor said at a normal volume, and they both *shush*ed her.

"Don't stare. And don't talk about them too loudly," Otto said. "That's how you stay safe."

"Talk about who?" Eleanor asked, bewildered and more than a little afraid. "Stay safe from what?"

"*Them*. The wrong things," Pip said. "Like the dog, but there are others, too. The dog is new. But there's other stuff."

"Like what?" Eleanor asked.

Pip hesitated. "I'm not sure we should tell you. It's safer if you don't notice them, and once someone tells you about them, it gets harder *not* to notice them. If they notice you noticing, or if someone overhears you talking about them . . ." She made a slicing motion over her throat.

"Don't listen to her," Otto said. He'd pulled a little bag of crumbs and birdseed out of his pocket and was making a small pile an arm's length away. Within seconds, two squirrels bounded across the courtyard and began snacking, apparently unconcerned that he was right there. "No one's going to kill you. But nobody will believe you, either, and you don't want anyone thinking you're crazy."

"Millie Jenkins talked about the wrong things, and she disappeared," Pip said.

"Millie Jenkins moved to Cleveland," Otto said.

"Like *that* sounds real," Pip said, rolling her eyes. "The January Society got her."

"What's—" Eleanor began, but Otto cut her off with a shake of his head.

"We shouldn't talk about this now," he said. "Millie might have moved to Cleveland, but August *definitely* got sent to an inpatient clinic and given a bunch of really strong drugs to make him stop seeing things that no one else believed were there. Don't worry. We'll help you. But you can't go around looking right at wrong things and saying stuff in the middle of the school courtyard."

"You guys brought *me* here," Eleanor pointed out.

"Yeah, because it's our spot," Pip said. She jabbed her fork toward Eleanor's untouched tray. "Are you going to eat that?"

"Um. I guess not," Eleanor said. Pip, who had finished off her food while they talked, started in on Eleanor's. Something about it made Eleanor's stomach give a happy flip. Like once someone stole food from you, you were destined to be friends.

She hadn't realized until she met Otto and Pip how much she wanted a friend. She'd thought she'd walled off that part of her, after the fire. But there it was.

She chewed the edge of her lip. A logical, rational part of her brain told her that none of this could be real. But a more rational part pointed out that if that was true, Pip and Otto couldn't have known what she saw.

"I used to see things like that. When I was little," she said. "But I stopped seeing them a long time ago. I thought I was done with all of it."

"It's Eden Eld," Pip said. "There's weird wrong stuff everywhere, but there's *tons* of it in Eden Eld."

"We don't know why," Otto said. "I've tried to track the frequency so I can form a proper hypothesis, but it's hard to gather data on other locations when my family only takes one vacation a year to Pasadena to visit my grandma."

"So all we've got is 'Eden Eld is weirder than other places,'" Pip concluded.

Eleanor thought. She stared off into the distance, and though her thoughts wanted to race, she forced herself to think slowly. Think carefully.

She wanted to be normal. She'd been oh so careful. But this—

If this was real? If this was true? If Otto and Pip saw the things she saw, if they could find answers or reasons or even just be in it together, that was a hundred times better than *normal*.

"You said you wanted to see Ashford House, right?" she said.

"Yeah?" Otto replied, already smiling. The squirrels had finished their meal and scurried away with satisfied squeaks.

"So come over after school. We can talk there, without anyone overhearing. You can tell me about the—the wrong things," Eleanor said.

"We can give you the crash course," Pip said with an enthusiastic nod.

"And you can give us the grand tour," Otto added.

"Deal," Eleanor said. She shook Otto's hand, then Pip's.

She'd made two friends in her first week. Aunt Jenny would be so pleased.

Six

At the end of the day, Pip got on the bus with Eleanor and Otto, and the bus driver didn't protest. "Don't you need a pass or something?" Eleanor asked.

Pip shrugged. "My mom's the headmistress. I get away with basically anything. Everybody's terrified of her, and she doesn't really care what I do. So it works out okay."

"My parents practice free-range parenting," Otto said, shaking his head so his hair flipped out from in front of his eye. It flopped right back again, but he seemed satisfied with the operation. "Also, I have triplet two-year-old siblings and seventeen pets, plus the ones I'm helping my dad rehabilitate. It creates a sort of protective chaos, especially since my older sister's off at college. I've got at least a couple hours before anyone notices I'm gone."

They sat crammed together on a bench really meant for only two people. Eleanor sat squished against the window, Pip squeezed in the middle, and Otto balanced on the edge. Eleanor watched the morning's landscape slide by in reverse as they chatted about some kind of seventh-grade drama that had unfolded after lunch. It was amazing to Eleanor that they could focus on that kind of thing. Could they be pulling her leg about the wrong things and the dog and all the rest?

Trees gave way to meadows and back to trees again. And there, in the shadows beneath the branches, was the dog from earlier. Big red eyes, mist falling from between his yellow teeth. Eleanor's hands went icy cold.

"Guys!" Eleanor said, and pointed. Pip craned around her, but they were already past.

"What is it?" Otto asked, half standing in his seat and trying to look through the rear window, which was hopelessly grimy.

"The dog," Eleanor said.

"Yeah, it's been showing up for like a week," Pip said. Her eyes darted around the bus, checking for eavesdroppers. "But seriously, keep your voice down."

"Usually the wrong things stick to one place, but it's been following us around. Maybe other people, too, but you can't exactly ask," Otto whispered. "Pip thinks we should try to attack it."

"I said we *could* try to attack it. Not *should*," Pip said.

"Your exact words were 'Just let me at it,'" Otto said.

Eleanor shivered. She was cold all the way through now. All the way to her heart, which seemed to beat so hard she could feel it in the tips of her shoulders.

"It hasn't done anything to us," Otto said. "It just watches. Maybe it's been there all along. Maybe we just didn't notice it until now."

"We usually notice the wrong things, though," Pip said, sounding disturbed by this idea.

"Not always. You didn't notice the whirly light until I showed you, and that was right outside your house."

Eleanor thought of the clock in the hall. The clock she had not seen until yesterday morning. Or had she?

She frowned and shut her eyes and thought about coming up the spiral staircase the day she arrived, her sad little duffel bag of everything she owned under her arm. She'd looked down the long hall and counted the doors. Three on the left. Four on the right. And across from the room where she'd sleep—the clock.

She was sure of it. It had been there all along. She just hadn't noticed.

She opened her eyes, still frowning. "There's something you guys have got to see when we get to the house," she said.

FROM THE OUTSIDE, Ashford House looked like a haunted mansion by way of Dr. Seuss. A turret stuck up on the west side of the house, like it had been pilfered from a medieval castle and attached with glue and possibly duct tape. The house was studded irregularly with round windows and square windows and rectangular windows and arched windows and even a triangular window, tucked up under the eaves.

Rooms and wings and awnings stuck out of it randomly, added on after it was built in the 1880s by Bartimaeus Ashford. The Ashford family had lived in the house all the way until the 1970s, when Eleanor's grandparents had moved in. Her grandparents had a lot of money for some reason Eleanor wasn't really clear on, and it had all gone away for reasons she was even *less* clear on. Jenny and Ben just had the house and Ben's job, and whatever Jenny made from selling her paintings, which wasn't much. Ben did what he could to keep up the house on the weekends, but there were shingles missing and windows cracked, and random boards and bits of metal heaped up near the side of the yard.

"Sorry it's kind of a mess," Eleanor said, feeling embarrassed even though she had nothing to do with the state of the house.

"I like it," Pip said. "It's scrappy. Everything in Eden Eld is so perfect. I've never even seen moss growing on a roof."

"Yeah, it's cool," Otto agreed. "It has *character*. All the houses in town look the same."

"Cookie cutter," Pip concurred, and they both nodded, like that settled the matter.

Eleanor led Pip and Otto up the drive to the winding concrete walkway that led to the front door, which was made from a big slab of wood full of knots and whorls and had an iron knob shaped like a rose.

Gray paw prints dotted the concrete, like a cat had tracked

dirt right up to the stoop. The paw prints hitched back and forth a few times and then trailed off into the grass.

"Big cat," Otto said.

Eleanor nudged one of the paw prints with the tip of her shoe. It smeared. Not like dirt at all; more like ash. "We don't have a cat," she said. "Must be a stray." She shivered even as she said it.

Aunt Jenny was in the drawing room (because Ashford House was the sort of place that had a drawing room). Jenny used it as a second studio for her painting, since the sun came in just right in the mornings, flooding the room with light, but in the past few weeks Jenny's fingers had started hurting too much to paint, and she couldn't sit in one place for long, either. Now she was lying back on the couch, half a dozen pillows propping her up as she talked on the phone.

"Yeah, but they say it can last for days like this. My mom was in early labor with Claire for two weeks."

Eleanor squeaked a floorboard, and Jenny looked up, a guilty expression flitting over her face. Because she'd mentioned Eleanor's mom, Eleanor knew. Jenny quickly smoothed the expression into a smile—a smile that grew bigger when she saw Pip and Otto hovering behind her.

"I'll call you back, Lena. Eleanor just got home." She hung up and levered herself into a more upright position, groaning and putting both hands on either side of her big belly. "How was your second day? I see you picked up some souvenirs."

"It was fine. This is Otto. And Pip. They're going to help me catch up with some schoolwork. Since I started so late." Once you told a big lie, telling smaller ones was easy. It got easier than telling the truth. Sometimes Eleanor had to stop herself from lying about things that didn't matter at all.

"That's lovely." Jenny grimaced suddenly.

"Are you okay?" Eleanor asked.

"It's just the baby," Aunt Jenny said, patting her big belly. "Contractions."

"Does that mean you have to go to the hospital?" Eleanor asked with alarm, heart giving a sloshy thump. "I can call Uncle Ben. I—"

Aunt Jenny shook her head. "Not yet, hon. Not until they're much stronger and much closer together. Don't you worry."

"Can we get you anything?" Otto asked. "A hot pack? Ice pack? Ice water? More pillows?" He sized up her pile of pillows with a practiced eye and didn't seem impressed. Triplet toddlers, Eleanor remembered.

"Oh, no. I'll haul myself upright in a few minutes," Aunt Jenny said, waving a hand. The gesture startled Eleanor—something about that tiny movement was so much like her mother, her chest gave a painful squeeze. She'd never realized how much her mother and Aunt Jenny were alike, before now. She'd never really gotten to know Jenny, because Eleanor's mother refused to bring her to Eden Eld. She'd only seen Jenny when she came to visit them, which wasn't very often.

When she did, she and Eleanor's mother always fought. Eleanor wasn't sure exactly why. It had something to do with their parents, and how her mother hadn't gone back for their funerals—but it was more than that, too.

Eleanor took the others to the back of the house—there were two sections of the third floor, and they didn't connect at all, which meant you had to use the back staircase to get to her room. Pip and Otto ooh-ed and aah-ed at the wood paneling and the antique wallpaper and the big, dusty chandeliers, and raced each other up the spiral staircase.

Eleanor had almost expected the big clock to be gone, or for Otto and Pip to not see it. Instead they all lined up in front of it, watching it *tick tock tick* backward as steadily as it had that morning.

"It's like it's counting down," Otto said.

Eleanor nodded. "But counting down to what?"

"I don't think I want to know the answer to that," Pip said.

"If you don't know, you can't make an informed decision," Otto said.

"You're always so *you*," Pip replied with a sigh, and Otto punched her arm affectionately.

"Is the clock a—a wrong thing?" Eleanor asked.

Pip and Otto frowned at each other. "I suppose," Otto said. "But usually the wrong things are less . . ."

"They're more . . ." Pip said at the same time.

"More frightening," Otto said.

"Less sitty," Pip said.

"That's not a word," Otto said.

"Is too, because I said it," Pip shot back. She folded her arms. "I suppose it's acting like wrong things, with the nobody-noticing bit. But usually wrong things give you the shivers and make your stomach pinch up. They make you want to stay away. The clock's strange, but it doesn't feel wrong."

"So what *are* the wrong things?" Eleanor asked.

"Some people seem to see them. Most people don't. Mostly we think it's kids that see them. Or that aren't smart enough to pretend they don't," Otto said. "They're all over Eden Eld. Like the whirly light—it kept trying to lead us out into the woods once we'd seen it. And there's a woman who walks down the middle of Bleecker Street sometimes."

"What's so weird about that?" Eleanor asked. "Other than not liking sidewalks?"

"She's *super* dead," Pip said. "See-through and everything. Her hair floats like she's underwater. But she doesn't hurt people. Hardly any of them *do* anything. They're just around. But it's not going to stay that way."

"You don't know that," Otto said.

"I do," Pip insisted. "Something bad's coming. The dog's been watching us, and my mom is *planning* something. And like I said: She's evil. Pretty sure she has flying monkeys hidden somewhere in a storage closet."

"You don't really believe that," Eleanor said.

"Of course I do. Haven't you been listening?" Pip said with a laugh. "Trust me. There's something evil coming for Eden Eld. For us. And soon. I feel it in my bones."

"If you believed that, you'd be scared," Eleanor said levelly. "You'd be terrified. You wouldn't be having fun."

"I am scared," Pip said. Her voice was suddenly quiet. "There are things about this town . . ." She drew in a deep breath and looked at Otto.

Otto's face was serious. "We've gotten used to joking around," he said. "We always have to make it sound like we're joking, in case someone hears. But Pip is right. Eden Eld is full of the wrong things, but they've been changing. They've been . . . watching us."

"We were starting to think we were both seeing things," Pip said. "Or making it all up until we believed it. But you're here. You're proof. You're like us."

The clock struck four. They jumped, all three of them at the same time, and then let out a chorus of nervous laughter.

"You're taking this really well," Otto said.

Eleanor bit her lip. "I told you. I've seen things like that before," she said. "There was this man . . ." She trailed off. She didn't want to talk about the man with see-through skin and shining bones. He hadn't done anything to her. He'd sat down next to her at a bus stop and opened a newspaper. The paper was covered in angry little black slashes instead of words. The photo on the front showed a line of people with empty holes for eyes, glaring at her.

He'd gotten on the bus. She'd stayed where she was, teeth chattering. She'd never told a soul.

"A ghost?" Pip guessed. Eleanor nodded, glad she didn't have to explain.

"Hey," Otto said excitedly. He was staring into the clock's glass case, where the pendulum swung to and fro in its steady, unrelenting rhythm. "There's something in there. There's something inside the clock."

Seven

Pip and Eleanor peered into the clock, propping their hands up to shade the glass so they could see past their reflections.

"There, in the corner," Otto said. "On the back."

"I see it," Eleanor said at once.

The back panel of the clock didn't fit quite right against the bottom left corner of the case, and something pale stuck out through the gap. Eleanor shooed Pip out of the way and opened the glass door. She reached under the swing of the pendulum, feeling along the wood panel. Her fingers touched the rough surface of old, thick paper, folded over. She tugged on it, and it slid reluctantly free, making the wood creak.

The paper had been folded once, twice, and three times, making a bulky packet. The creases cracked as she smoothed it out in her hands and read it out loud.

Thirteen tales and thirteen keys,
Prowling beasts that no one sees.

Three are marked in flesh and name,
This way, that way, both the same.
A bargain struck in days of yore,
Thirteen keys, but just one door.
All Hallows' Eve is when he'll come.
When clock strikes twelve, you'd better run.

The left-hand edge of the page was ragged, like it had been torn from a book. At the bottom of the page was a little symbol, a peculiar curlicue hooked through the eye of an old-fashioned key.

Eleanor's hand shook. Thirteen tales.

"What does it mean?" Otto asked. "What tales? What keys?"

"I'm more worried about the beasts," Pip said.

"I know what this is from," Eleanor whispered.

"All Hallows' Eve—that's Halloween," Otto said.

"That's *Saturday*," Pip replied.

"I know what this is from," Eleanor said again, loudly this time, and they stared at her. She tried to put the words together to explain, but all that came out was an empty puff of breath and a little click in the back of her throat. She knelt instead, pulling her backpack around to the front of her body. She unzipped the bag with one hand, still clutching the poem in the other, and pulled out the book.

Thirteen Tales of the Gray. The book was thin. A hardback, with the old-fashioned kind of cloth cover, bumpy and textured with ash still worked into the weave. Embossed on the cover, beneath the title and above *Collected by B. A.*, was the same symbol from the page. A curlicue and a key.

"Where did you get that?" Pip asked.

"It was my mother's," Eleanor said. "She used to read it to me every night, when I was little. When I used to see the wrong things. But she stopped when I stopped seeing." Or had it been the other way around?

Eleanor opened the book to the first page. The spine cracked. The pages were brittle and thin, rippled toward the edges, and they'd turned a shade of brown that made her think of old libraries and desperately want a cup of cocoa and a fire to read next to. She had always wondered why the first page was torn out, but her mother said it must have happened before she got it.

The poem fit perfectly against the ragged edge inside.

"Whoa," Pip said.

"Whoa," Otto agreed, nodding. "Oh, look." He pointed at the inside cover. In careful block letters, someone had written *Property of Andy Ashford*.

"Ashford? Like this house," Eleanor said. She didn't really remember seeing that before, but her mother had always been the one to hold the book and read the stories. "Maybe she found it here when she was a kid."

She flipped forward, carefully turning the torn page. The next page was blank, and the one after that just had the title and the author again, but then there was a table of contents, listing each of the stories.

"It's kind of a weird book," she said. She frowned. She

couldn't remember *why* it had always seemed so strange. She couldn't remember the stories at all, but she remembered her mother's voice, and she remembered the harsh ink strokes of the illustrations. And there was something else . . . "The stories are weird, but that's not all. It says there are thirteen tales, but there are actually only twelve. See?" She pointed to the table of contents, laboriously counting them again and again.

The People Who Look Away

The Glass-Heart Girl

Rattlebird

Iron, Ash, and Salt

The Orchard Thieves

Jack and the Hungry House

Cat-of-Ashes

The Brackenbeast

The Kindly Dark

Tatterskin

The Girl Who Danced with the Moon

The Graveyard Dog

"Are those fairy tales?" Pip asked. "I've never heard of any of them. And I've read, like, hundreds. My dad translates them from all over the world."

"Wait. There are thirteen," Otto said.

"No, that's twelve," Eleanor said, frowning. She counted again, but she remembered asking her mother about it, and her mother didn't know either. "The last one is 'The Graveyard Dog.'"

"But there's something written beneath it," Otto said. He pointed, resting the tip of his finger against the page. And he was right. There *was* something written there—but it was like the letters had faded into the page. Or were still in the process of appearing. Eleanor couldn't make it out.

"This has to mean something," she said. "The clock. The book. The poem. We found them for a reason, and it has to do with the wrong things." She spoke as if it were fact, waiting to see if it sounded wrong. But it sounded right, and Otto and Pip were nodding.

"But *what* does it mean?" Pip asked.

Eleanor ran her finger over the little curlicue and the key at the bottom of the page. It was exactly the same as the keys that were painted around the clock face. The same as the mark on her wrist. "I think it has to do with me," she said softly, and pulled up her sleeve to show them.

Otto and Pip stared at the birthmark on her wrist. And then they looked at each other.

Pip pulled down the collar of her shirt. Otto hiked up the hem of his jacket. Two keys: one just above Pip's collarbone, the other on Otto's right hip.

"I think," Otto corrected softly, "it's about *us*."

Eleanor gulped. *Us*. She'd felt it when she touched them, before they even met properly—they were connected. She wasn't sure if that made her feel better or more afraid. Either way, she was glad not to be alone.

She glanced down the hall. It made her feel antsy being

out in the open like this. "Let's go back to my room," she said, and marched her way to the door without waiting for an answer. She sat on the end of her bed. Pip flopped down next to her, propped up on her elbows, and Otto took the chair by the desk.

"Okay. Obviously we need to investigate and figure out exactly what's going on here. We should look at the poem again," Otto suggested. "We need to analyze it."

"We're wasting time," Pip argued. " 'You'd better run.' That sounds pretty bad. We should be getting ready to fight."

"Fight what, though?" Otto asked. "We need to slow down and examine the evidence!"

"We need to find weapons. And escape routes," Pip said. "Something's coming. I can *feel* it."

"You're both right," Eleanor said, and their attention snapped back to her. "What we need is a plan. And a good plan has two parts. Gathering information, and acting on it. We need to do both, and we need to do it fast. So let's look at what we know." She opened the book to the torn page. "Thirteen keys—there are twelve keys and a smudge on the clock, but we don't know what that means. Prowling beasts—that's got to be the dog. And the bird."

"Bird?" Otto asked, and she explained about the thing she'd seen in the tree.

"Then it says, 'Three are marked in flesh and name,'" Pip said. "The birthmarks?"

"But what about the name part?" Otto asked. They looked

at each other, but no one had a suggestion, so Eleanor shrugged and moved on.

"Um. 'A bargain struck,' and then the keys again. We don't know any of that yet. And then Halloween . . . That must be when something is supposed to happen. But we don't know what."

"Maybe the stories can tell us," Pip suggested.

Eleanor ran her finger along the edge of the page, oddly reluctant to open it. The stories had always belonged to her and her mother, just the two of them. But if she was going to share them with anyone, it felt right that it was Otto and Pip.

"The first story," she said, trying to remember. "The first story is about a kingdom, long ago." She turned the pages. There was the title, and beneath it the black-and-white drawing of a castle, overgrown with vines and thorns, vultures circling overhead. She took a deep breath, and, her mother's voice echoing in her mind, began to read.

Eight

The People Who Look Away

Once there was a kingdom, and the kingdom was dying. Crops withered in the fields. Animals grew ill and died. The people were sick and starving, and they cried to their king to help them. Some said the king was a good man and some said he was a wicked man. Whether he was good or bad, though, he was a frightened man. For he had so very much, and his people had so very little, and while he wished that they had more, most of all he feared that he would have less.

And so he sent word to every corner of the world that if someone could find a way to save his kingdom, he would grant them anything they asked.

The word passed from town to town and kingdom to kingdom, across the whole of the world and beyond it. It reached dark and hidden places, lost places, forgotten places, where words were only whispered and what heard them wasn't human at all.

Three people answered his call and came to the court. They were odd travelers, dressed strangely, in the garb of another land or another time. They said they were siblings, two sisters and their brother, who came to solve the riddle of the dying kingdom. The man was the strangest of all, with gray, quick eyes that seemed to hold a hundred secrets, and three strange beasts he kept as companions: a great cat that smelled of ash and smoke, a bird whose wing-beats rattled like bones, and a huge dog, a black beast with eyes like the coals of a fire . . .

Eleanor stopped reading. She ran her fingertip under the words.

"That's him," Pip said, sitting up. "That's the dog we saw."

Eleanor went back to the list of stories, and her eye caught on the last one. She flipped ahead. There he was again, staring out of an illustration. The drawing was black and white, but it looked like his eyes were glowing. "Look," she said, showing the others, and they pressed into either side of her as she skimmed the story of the graveyard dog. The story didn't have anything to do with Eden Eld—it was about a brother and a sister whose stepmother threw them out of their house, and who slept in a graveyard by accident. They defeated the dog with an iron shovel and then were rewarded with a bunch of treasure. But she was absolutely sure it was the same dog.

"Read the rest," Pip whispered. Their voices had dropped to a hush, caught in the spell of the story. Eleanor was remembering a bit more with every word. Now she read confidently, as if she knew the words before she spoke them.

The strange man offered the king a bargain: he would grant the kingdom great wealth and prosperity. The treasure vaults would burst with gold. The fields would flourish. The rivers would flow but never flood. No building would fall, no knife would dull, no stone would crack. And for all of this, he asked only one thing: in thirteen years, the man would return and ask for a single treasure, the most valuable thing the king possessed.

This seemed an easy deal for the king. If his treasure vaults were full, he would hardly miss one bauble, even if it were the grandest he owned. But his sister, whose mother had been a wise woman of the old sort, the sort with secret knowledge and a keen eye, told him not to take the bargain. The man was some kind of wicked spirit or warlock, she warned, and no good would come of his deal.

The king waved aside her worries. It was a small price to pay, he said, and agreed.

The man smiled. His sisters smiled, too, but the cat looked at the king's sister as if to say she was right. And then all of them vanished.

For thirteen years, the kingdom did flourish. There was plenty to eat. The sun shone, the rivers flowed, the animals were hearty and healthy. A new sort of flower even began to bloom in the kingdom, and the people called it the Promise Flower, for the promise of prosperity the strange man had made. And even in the autumn and through the coldest winters the flowers bloomed: proof, it seemed, that the bargain held.

Now, just after the bargain was struck, the king had a daughter. Her name was Rose, and though he had never before loved anything that wasn't his fastest horse or his most glittering gem or his shiniest piece of gold, he loved her, and he found himself suddenly uninterested in the treasures that filled his vaults. He no longer spent his days hunting in the forest with his hounds, but in the nursery, doting on the little princess.

On her thirteenth birthday, a visitor came to court. The king had almost forgotten, but he welcomed the strange man with open arms. "Come," he said. "The treasure vaults are bursting; take your pick, and let the bargain be fulfilled."

But the strange man smiled. "That is not your greatest treasure," he said, and his eyes turned toward the princess. And the cat looked at the king's sister, as if to say, You were right.

The king went pale. He refused. The man insisted. The king offered gold and jewels. The man stood firm. And finally, in a rage, the king ordered him thrown from the castle. He would not give up his child.

The man only smiled and went on his way, and the king thought that was the end of that. The people waited for the kingdom to fall again into ruin, but things continued as they always had. The flowers bloomed. And, in time, the day came for the princess to be married.

Of all her suitors, one was the finest: the most handsome, the strongest, the wealthiest, the most learned. He serenaded her with song and flattered her father and granted gifts from strange and distant places that dazzled everyone—everyone except the king's sister, who did not like the look of him at all.

But the princess was smitten, and so, it must be said, was the *king. They held a lavish wedding, full of dance and laughter and music, but the king's sister was still suspicious. She scattered flour on the ground where the bride and groom would walk, and crept behind them as they passed. And she saw that the man's footprints were pointing the wrong way.*

She knew at once that the prince was the man who had come all those years ago, and she knew who he and his strange sisters were: the People Who Look Away, the worst of tricksters and spirits, who sneak through the cracks in the world to ensnare people with their bargains.

She raised an alarm, and the castle's guards raced into the princess and her husband's wedding chamber. But the man was gone, and so were his sisters—and so was the princess. All the king's soldiers searched from town to town and kingdom to kingdom, but the princess was never found.

Months later, a child appeared in front of the castle gates. A baby girl. She looked just like the missing princess, save for one thing: her hands were turned the wrong way around, her palms facing outward instead of in.

The story ended there, without another word.

Eleanor had read the old versions of many fairy tales. The versions where witches danced in iron shoes until they died or were rolled off cliffs in barrels. The versions where even the happy endings were vicious things full of revenge and blood. She found them interesting, and sometimes more fun, and sometimes horrible—like when you could tell that whoever came up with the story didn't think very well of girls.

But none of them just ended like that.

The illustration on the last page showed the king's sister stooping to look at the footprints in the flour. She held something up to her eye, like a crystal or a piece of glass, and was peering through it. The caption said *The Trick Revealed*. And just beneath it, someone had inked, with a ballpoint pen: *Mr. January*.

Who's Mr. January? she remembered asking her mother.

I don't know, she'd answered. *It was written in there when I found it.*

Found it. Not *got* it or *bought* it, but *found* it. Here in Ashford House.

"January," Pip said, stabbing her finger at the note. She was still lying on her stomach, while Eleanor sat cross-legged beside her on the bed. "Like the January Society."

"That doesn't prove anything," Otto said, somewhat skeptically. He'd come to stand at Eleanor's elbow, leaning over a little, his fingers fidgeting like he wanted to ask to hold the book but wasn't sure he should.

"They're evil," Pip replied stubbornly.

"You keep talking about the January Society, but I still don't know what they are," Eleanor said.

"It's a group for the descendants of the original town founders. They're just a social club," Otto said.

"Nuh-uh. They're evil, and my mom's their secret evil leader."

"Everyone thinks their parents are evil," Otto said.

Eleanor curled her fingers tighter, until her nails dug into her palms. *Her* mother wasn't evil. She was sick.

But she supposed her father could be evil. She'd never met him. She didn't even know his name.

"My parents actually *are* evil, though," Pip said. Eleanor couldn't tell if she was serious or playing around. Maybe both. It was safer to joke, she thought. It was safer to pretend it wasn't real. "They skulk around and have secret meetings and talk in code. And they've got all this weird old stuff."

"The January Society's meetings aren't secret, they're just private. And it's a boring fundraising organization. Also, if antique collecting makes you evil, my great-aunt Prudence is *definitely* evil," Otto said. He almost sounded like he was enjoying himself now. "But Pip's *obsessed*. She bought all this 'spy gear' online so she could catch them summoning demons or something, but *mysteriously* she hasn't found anything."

"Not true. Once I caught them lighting candles and holding hands over a weird table. Like it was an altar. Like they were casting spells," Pip continued. "They were wearing these big black robes with hoods."

"You were probably dreaming. And anyway, that doesn't make you evil. My sister's girlfriend is Wiccan, and she only does spells to feel confident and wish luck on people and stuff," Otto said.

"Ugh. Otto. Can you just let me finish?" Pip asked.

"Just playing Scully to your Mulder," he said.

"Double ugh. Why do you have to watch such old shows?"

"*X-Files* is classic."

"You're classic."

"What is that even supposed to mean?" Otto asked, laughing, and they grinned at each other.

Eleanor found herself smiling a little. Not because it was funny, and not because she felt in on the joke, but because they obviously liked each other so much, and knew each other so well. She couldn't remember the last time she had friends like that. It was like smelling food and suddenly realizing how hungry you were.

Pip's expression got serious. "I know we joke around a lot," she said. "But Otto, I'm serious. I don't trust them. And my mom is . . . You know how she is."

"She can't be evil," Otto said. "She's not the nicest person ever, but she's your *mom*."

"It's easy for you to say when your parents are so perfect," Pip replied.

"They're not perfect," Otto said, but he made it sound like they weren't far off from perfect, either.

"Well, I don't know anything about the January Society. And we don't know who wrote that in the book," Eleanor said. "But I think we need to—"

There was a scratching sound above them, and then a scrape and something else—a rattle. A hollow, clacking sound. Something on the roof. They all stared up. Eleanor closed the book

and pulled it against her chest as if to protect it. *Clackclackclack.*
Clackclackclack.

Then there was a croak, and a great flapping of wings, and the rasping, rattling sound moved quickly away.

"Rattlebird," Pip whispered. "I think we're being watched."

Nine

They listened for the rattlebird—if that was what it was—but heard nothing more. They clustered together on the floor at the foot of the bed and dropped their voices to whispers.

"We need to make a plan," Eleanor said.

"We need to know what we're up against," Pip replied. "And what the January Society is up to. We should go back to my house. I've got tons of spy gear."

"I don't know. The answer's got to be in the book," Eleanor said. "We should read every story. And look at the pictures, too. There are clues in there, I know it."

"Maybe we should—" Otto began, but then there was a knock on the door. They all jumped guiltily, and Eleanor shoved the book under the bed just before the door opened and Ben stuck his head in.

"Oh, hello," he said, sounding pleasantly surprised to find them there, though Jenny must have told him where they were.

Ben was a burly man with a bushy beard and hair that was going a bit thin on top even though he wasn't very old. He was a writer, but that didn't pay very well, so he also worked construction in town and did odd jobs. A lot of odd jobs now, since they were trying to save up for the baby.

"Hi, Uncle Ben," she said. "These are—"

"Pip and Otto," he said, pointing finger guns at each of them in turn. "I got the skinny from your aunt. Anyhoo, dinner's ready if you're hungry."

"Dinner? But it's only—" Eleanor jumped as the clock in the hall chimed out the hour. Six o'clock. She'd lost track of time.

"Clearly you're having too much fun," Ben said. "You can fuel up, and then, Pip, your mom's coming to pick you up."

"My mom?" Pip said, voice a squeak.

"Unless I talked to an imposter," he said with a chuckle, then wrinkled his forehead when none of them so much as cracked a smile. "Anyway, food's downstairs."

Pip looked at each of them. Eleanor raised her shoulder in a half shrug. What could they do? And Otto was right—they didn't have proof that Pip's mom was evil, or that the January Society was anything other than a charity organization. But still . . .

"Uncle Ben, could Otto and Pip spend the night?"

"Oh. Um." He scratched his chin. "Leaping ahead in my expected parental decision-making by a decade or so here, but let's see." He thought it over, then shook his head. "Nope, can't do it. School night."

"But—"

"Sorry, kiddo," he said. "But let's make a plan for Friday?"

Eleanor sighed. There was no way to explain so that he would understand. "Friday would be great."

Ben clapped his hands together. "Fantastic. Now scurry on down those stairs. Wait too long, and I might eat your share."

He turned and ambled down the hall, whistling.

"How did your mom even know we were here?" Otto asked Pip.

"She must have installed another one of those tracker apps on my phone," Pip said. It could have been evil. Or it could have just been helicopter parenting. The three of them trudged downstairs.

Jenny had made pasta, which mostly meant thawing the sauce that Ben had made a few nights before. Jenny didn't do much cooking, since she couldn't reach the back burners anymore.

"So. You three already seem thick as thieves," Jenny said while they ate. Ashford House had a dining room, but the table was so huge you couldn't even reach across it to pass the butter, so they always ate in the kitchen. "What were you up to upstairs?"

Otto's eyes widened a little, nervousness radiating from him, but Eleanor answered immediately. "Homework," she said.

"I hope they're not loading you up with too much right away," Ben said.

"No, but there's a lot of catching up to do so I know what's going on," Eleanor lied smoothly. Pip gave her an impressed look. Otto stared intently at his pasta.

"It's good that you have help, then," Jenny said. She smiled at Pip and Otto, who did their best to look virtuous. "So, Pip, you're Delilah's daughter?"

"You know her?" Pip said.

"Sort of," Jenny said. "She was more my sister's friend than mine. There's a big age gap between us. But I knew she had a kid Eleanor's age. I'm so glad that you three are spending time together." She didn't sound just glad—she was beaming. She'd been so worried that Eleanor would have trouble starting at a new school this late in the year.

Whatever Pip's suspicions about her parents, Jenny and Ben had nothing to do with what was going on. Eleanor was sure of it. And she was sure that they would help, if they could. However clever three twelve-year-olds might be, they needed adult help.

"Aunt Jenny," she said cautiously, not wanting to plunge in too quickly. "Was there always a clock in the hall outside my room?"

Otto widened his eyes at her. Pip shook her head in tiny, quick movements. Ben and Jenny glanced at each other, faintly puzzled. "Clock?" Ben asked.

Eleanor's mouth was dry, her nerves buzzing, but she forced herself to sound only mildly curious. "Yeah. An old grandfather clock. Very fancy," Eleanor said. Pip was slicing her hand over her throat in a "stop now" gesture, leaning back so Jenny and Ben couldn't see.

"Are you sure?" Jenny asked.

"I could show you," Eleanor said, though she wasn't honestly sure she could.

"No, wait. A clock. Yeah," Ben said, nodding slowly. "Sure. It's . . . It was your dad's, wasn't it?" he asked Jenny.

"Right," Jenny said, as if it was coming back to her. "Old family heirloom. Gosh. I can't believe I forgot it's up there. I must walk past it all the time to get to the upstairs bedrooms. Although I haven't spent much time on the third floor lately." She laughed a little and patted her belly.

"It's kind of strange, isn't it?" Eleanor pressed. "The way it runs backward?"

"It—what? Runs backward?" Jenny asked. Her brow was furrowed.

"The clock outside my room," Eleanor went on. Otto and Pip had looks of absolute horror on their faces.

"That's right. We were just talking about that," Jenny said.

Ben looked confused. "Yeah, we were. Weren't we? I totally forgot."

"Well," Jenny said. "Well—I—that is strange." She was frowning and shaking her head in this odd little motion, wagging to and fro, to and fro. Ben stared down at his plate with a big frown half hidden by his beard.

Pip clanged her fork loudly against her plate. "This is

delicious!" she declared. "I'm getting seconds. Ms. Barton, do you want more?"

"Oh! No thank you, dear," Jenny said, snapping back to cheerfulness. "There's not much room for my stomach these days. The little devil's really throwing out her elbows."

They didn't talk about the clock or much of anything else for the rest of the meal. Otto volunteered the three of them for dish duty, which Jenny was more than happy to put in their hands so she could go lie down again while Ben finished putting together the crib upstairs. With running water to help cover their voices, they leaned in together over the soapy sink.

"You can't tell people about the wrong things," Pip whispered.

"They aren't evil. They could help us," Eleanor said.

"They can't," Otto said solemnly.

"They acted so weird. Why did Aunt Jenny freak out like that? She was shaking," Eleanor said.

"Because she's not used to the wrong things. Her brain's learned not to see them, if it ever saw them at all," Otto said. "That's part of why you never, ever tell people about the wrong things. If they're not like us, they can get really strange. Hurt themselves, even."

"I tried to show my therapist that there was a door in his ceiling and he had a seizure," Pip said matter-of-factly. Eleanor flushed. She didn't know anyone her age who had a therapist, other than herself. But Pip said it like it wasn't anything unusual.

Her mother hated psychologists and psychiatrists, but now Eleanor wondered if that was because she was afraid—afraid of what they might do if they found out about the things her mother saw. The things she saw, too.

Pip went on. "Mostly, people just forget right after. But if you really want to get them to see without hurting them, you have to hint at it. Kind of trick them into seeing out of the corners of their eyes and build up to it. But it's usually not a good idea. And even if you manage it, they don't remember for very long."

"We've done lots of experiments." Otto nodded.

"But then someone decided it was unethical to test human subjects without board oversight," Pip said with a roll of her eyes. "Like there's a wrong things science board."

Pip's phone buzzed, and they all jumped. Pip pulled it out of her pocket. It had to be a brand-new phone—it was the latest model, which hadn't been out long at all—but a crack already ran down the center of the screen. She had a text from a number listed as MOMBEAST: *Three-minute warning.*

"I guess that's it," Pip said.

"It's okay," Otto said. "We can talk more tomorrow. Figure all this out."

"I'll read the book tonight," Eleanor said. "Cover to cover." It wasn't much of a sacrifice. Staying up late to read was the one thing that was always worth getting into trouble for.

"But what does the book have to do with *us*?" Otto asked.

"What does it have to do with *here*? I don't think we're going to find everything we need in the book."

"The wrong things happen more in Eden Eld. And we're all here," Eleanor said. "I think we need to know more about the town. The poem said '*a bargain struck in days of yore.*' So we should look at the history of Eden Eld."

"We can look in the town archive," Otto said, as if he'd just declared that they would be going to a candy store. "It's stored in the Academy library. We don't even have to leave school grounds."

"Perfect," Eleanor said. They looked at Pip expectantly.

"I suppose research is a good idea," she admitted. "But at some point we're going to need to actually *do* something. We have to know what we're going to do if we can't find the answers in time."

Just then, the doorbell rang.

Ten

They heard voices in the foyer and filed out to find Jenny talking to Ms. Foster. It might have been after hours, but she looked no less polished than she had in her office. More so, really, here in the slightly run-down old house.

She wore the Eden Eld–blue skirt suit. Silver cufflinks winked at the sleeves, but Eleanor couldn't quite make out their shape. When Ms. Foster saw the kids, she stepped away from Ben and Jenny, her perfect white teeth showing between her lips in what didn't quite qualify as a smile.

"Pip, love," she said in a voice like honeysuckle. The hairs on the back of Eleanor's neck stood up, but Ben and Jenny looked charmed as could be. "And Otto. Always such a pleasure to see you." She folded her hands in front of her and set her weight back like she was drinking in the sight of them. "And of course our newest pupil. I'm so glad you three are already getting to be such good friends. It's always hard to move to a new town.

Although Eden Eld isn't quite a new town, is it, Eleanor? You've got it in your blood."

Eleanor's mouth was dry. She wanted to shrink back and back and back until she vanished, but she held her ground.

Ms. Foster stepped forward, reaching up, and it took Eleanor every bit of control she had not to flinch away as she tucked a strand of Eleanor's hair behind her ear. Then she took Eleanor's hands in hers, looking into her eyes. "I hope you'll feel at home here in no time. You belong to this town," she said.

Pip's mother had cool, dry hands. They made Eleanor think of the time she got to hold a python. You could feel all its muscles beneath, getting ready to squeeze. Ms. Foster sighed. "You really are the spitting image of your mother."

Eleanor's stomach lurched. Her heart beat *whump-thump* and she felt it in her throat. But Ms. Foster didn't let go, and neither did she. "Yes, we look a lot alike," she said. She smiled. Puppet strings at the corners of her mouth. Wrinkles at the corners of her eyes.

"Well. We really must be going," Ms. Foster said, and dropped her hands at last. Before she did, Eleanor caught a glimpse of the cufflinks. Each one showed two bearded faces pointing in opposite directions, joined in the middle like they were the same man, the same head, but looking two ways at once.

It itched something in the back of her mind, but she couldn't place it.

"Would you like a ride home, Otto?" Ms. Foster asked.

He blanched, but then he caught Pip's eye. Eleanor could

guess what they were thinking. If Otto accepted the ride, at least they'd have longer together to look out for each other. Pip would have less time alone with her mother. And even if Ms. Foster wasn't evil—a possibility Eleanor was beginning to doubt, whatever Otto said—Eleanor didn't imagine it was fun, being her daughter.

"Thanks, Ms. Foster. That would be great," Otto said brightly. He turned and, before Eleanor could react, grabbed Eleanor in a hug. He whispered in her ear. "Read the book again. And be careful. Watch out for the dog and the rattlebird."

"You too," she said.

Pip waved glumly from behind her mother's back as they headed down the hall. Nothing would happen tonight, Eleanor told herself. Otto and Pip had been safe for nearly thirteen years in Eden Eld. They'd be safe for one more night.

She didn't really believe in *safe* anymore—it had gone to the same place *normal* had. But she was getting pretty good at lying to herself, too.

When the door shut, Aunt Jenny gave Eleanor a bright smile. "So. Friends already," she said, as pleased as Eleanor had known she would be.

"Yep," Eleanor said, managing to sound chipper. "They're great."

Jenny frowned. "Is something wrong, hon?" she asked. "You look worried."

Eleanor hesitated. They *would* help her if they could. But they couldn't, could they? And there was the baby—what if something happened to Jenny and the baby, and it was her fault? She needed to protect them. And protect herself, by herself.

"You can tell us anything, you know," Jenny said—and then she winced.

"Starting again?" Ben asked. His face was screwed up like he was feeling sympathetic and guilty that he couldn't take some of the discomfort for her, but also like he was really relieved he wasn't the one who had to do this part.

"You are changing *so many* diapers," she growled at him as she braced herself against the wall. A few seconds later she was panting but relaxed again. "Still not regular. We're fine," she assured him. "Could be days."

"Could be days," he echoed. He looked at Eleanor. "Sorry. What were we talking about?"

Eleanor couldn't put them in danger. Especially not with the baby on the way. "Nothing," she said. "It's not important."

"Okay. If you say so," Jenny said. "I think I'm going to go straight to bed."

"Need me to come rub your feet?" Ben asked.

"If you don't, they may fall off completely," Jenny told him, and he put his arm over her shoulders.

The way they moved, the way they touched each other, you could tell they loved each other more than anything. And they had for a long time. It was a little like watching Pip and Otto bicker affectionately, but different, too. Eleanor didn't need to be part of their closeness. But it felt like standing next to a stove on a winter day. It made you warm, just by being close to it.

Eleanor went to her room, locked the door, and sat in the armchair near the window, cracking open the book of stories. She started at the beginning again, with "The People Who Look Away," and read through every line. Every page.

When she was done, she turned back to the beginning and started again.

SHE DREAMED OF smoke, and of her mother's hands on her arms. *Whatever you do, don't go back to Eden Eld,* she shouted. *Thirteens—it's all thirteens.*

Then her mother was gone. The smoke and fire were all around her, and she couldn't move. She was too afraid. She couldn't breathe. She choked and coughed. Through the smoke she saw the shape of a man—a man in an old-fashioned suit, facing away from her. Then, slowly, he started to turn.

Eleanor woke with a start in the chair with her arm asleep, pinched under her, her glasses squashed uncomfortably where her cheek leaned against the chair, and the clock in the hall striking ten. It was an odd and mournful sound, especially in the dark, and it was strangely loud. It took her a moment to realize why. Her bedroom door was open.

She had definitely closed it. She had definitely locked it. So how had it come open? She leaned over and turned on the light beside her bed. The darkness seemed to push back at it, and it illuminated the room only faintly.

There were paw prints on her floor, gray and sooty. A cat's paws, but big, bigger than any she'd seen. They marched across the floor and right out the door. An ashy paw print marked the doorframe, right next to the lock, as if the cat had propped itself on its hind legs for a moment.

Eleanor had fallen asleep reading the book. It was tucked down beside the arm of the chair. She walked to her bed and stowed it out of sight under the pillow, and then followed the paw prints into the hall, her breath fast and shallow and the hairs on the back of her arms prickling.

The footprints marched right to the spiral steps and down them. She inched down one step at a time, sticking to the outside of the curve so she could peer around the bend. The paw prints continued. Nothing else in the house moved.

She turned on lights as she went. Down to the first floor, down the hall. The paw prints got muddled here and there, where the cat peeked into rooms before backing out again, but they continued in the same general direction until they came to the living room. The living room was properly called the *great room*. There was also the drawing room, where Jenny painted in the mornings, and the den, where Ben and Jenny did most of their relaxing. The great room was just too big and cavernous to relax in, though it was very impressive. It had shelves that wrapped around three walls, reaching all the way to the edge of the humongous fireplace. The fireplace was big enough to walk into—even Ben could walk in without bending his head. There was a grate in the middle, but there was plenty of room to walk around the edge and get to the staircase that rose inexplicably behind the fireplace, leading up to a stone wall.

The paw prints went right into the fireplace.

Eleanor followed them, stepping softly so she wouldn't make a sound. The floorboards creaked anyway, but she hoped the settling and groaning of the house would cover them.

She reached the fireplace and peered up. The footprints pattered right up the steps, all the way to the wall—and stopped.

There was no cat. No anything. Just the paw prints on the top step.

Eleanor let out a breath. She wasn't sure if she was relieved or even more unsettled to find the top step empty. She walked up the steps and pushed on the wall. Solid stone. She pressed her ear against it and knocked. Was the sound hollow?

She couldn't tell.

She turned back around. The paw prints were flaking away, vanishing as if scattered by the wind, but there wasn't so much as a breeze. She followed them back the way she had come. By the time she got to her room, there was no sign of them.

She closed the door. Locked it. And turned around.

The book sat in the middle of her bed. It was open to an illustration in the middle of the book. The one for "Jack and the Hungry House." It showed Jack, his indispensable walking stick in hand. The girl with backward hands, who had showed up in several of the stories, was just visible at the door of the house, turned back like she was waiting for him. She held a rose in her left hand. It was the rose she used in the story to mark the shifting doors and halls in the hungry house, leaving petals for the safe ways to walk and thorns for the dangerous ones.

There was a figure Eleanor hadn't noticed before. A tiny, pale figure, more of an interruption in the lines that made the dark night sky than a proper shape. Only a few faint lines defined the figure's body. It was a man. He seemed to be wearing an old-fashioned kind of suit, and he was facing away from Jack.

Eleanor paged through the book, suspicion at the back of her mind. There was a figure there in the drawing in "Tatterskin," too, in one of the windows of the haunted town, facing away—a woman this time, tall and pale. And the man was in the ballroom in "The Girl Who Danced with the Moon." Two of them appeared in "The Kindly Dark," just shadows against the stars as Jack and the girl with backward hands fled the sunrise.

The only place she couldn't find any of the People Who Look Away in was the illustration from the first story, and the man's—Mr. January's?—footprints were in that one.

That illustration was on page 12. On page 13, the page number was underlined in pen. Eleanor frowned and flipped through again. Three numbers were underlined. Page 3 and page 13. And then page 133 had just the first two numbers underlined. 3, 13, 13. She whispered the numbers to herself so she was sure she would remember.

Three, thirteen, thirteen. It's all thirteens, she thought, and she drifted off to sleep.

Eleven

It was agony to wait through breakfast, and then the long ride to school, and then two whole periods before the lunch bell rang and they could bolt to the library together. Pip led the way past the fiction section to a heavy door marked ARCHIVE.

"It's not locked?" Eleanor asked.

"Doors don't usually *get* locked in Eden Eld," Pip said. "No one ever steals anything."

The room was crowded with metal shelves filled with cardboard boxes, glass cabinets, wooden bureaus with long, flat drawers, and stacks of old newspapers. A musty, dusty smell hung in the air. One of the lights in the back kept flickering before coming back on with a buzz, and a discarded diorama covered with illustrations of pea plants lay trampled on the floor.

"This," Pip declared with a flourish, "is the world's greatest repository of Eden Eld–related lore."

"It's the world's only repository of Eden Eld–related lore, since city hall flooded and they moved everything that didn't get destroyed here," Otto said.

Eleanor felt a little shiver of excitement. She loved old books and old records and anything that might qualify as an *artifact*. She felt like she was standing in the middle of a hundred little mysteries, and she had to remind herself there was only one that mattered right now. "Where do we even start?" she asked.

Pip looked at Otto. Otto looked at Eleanor. Eleanor glared.

"I asked first," she said.

"I guess we just pick a shelf and start reading," Otto said. "Not very scientific of us."

"We can narrow it down better than that," Eleanor said, more confidently than she felt. "Let's think about what we know. We have the poem and the book. There's the clock. And we all have the same birthmark."

"We're all from founding families," Pip said.

"Really?" Eleanor asked, surprised.

"Barton, Foster, Ellis," Pip said, pointing to each of them in turn. "There were thirteen founding families. I can recite them all, if you want."

"Thirteen," Eleanor said. *Thirteens. It's all thirteens.* "I'm almost thirteen years old."

"Me too," Pip said. "And Otto. We have the same birthday."

Eleanor's hands went cold. It couldn't be. "It isn't—your birthday isn't Halloween, is it?" she asked in a whisper. Pip and Otto nodded in unison. "Okay. *That's* spooky."

"All Hallows' Eve," Otto said. "We have the same birthmark and we're all turning thirteen on All Hallows' Eve? Whatever's happening, it's happening *tomorrow*."

"Then we need to work fast," Eleanor said. "Spread out. Look for anything about Halloween and the town's history."

"And the January Society," Pip added.

"And the January Society," Eleanor agreed. "That should narrow it down."

She started sorting through old newspapers, trying to find ones from October of years past. She'd barely fished one out—October 26, 1993—when Otto made a triumphant noise.

"Guys! Look at this," he said excitedly, and Eleanor felt a thudding sense of disappointment that she hadn't been the one to find something. She shoved the feeling away. Otto held out a magazine, flipped to a page in the middle. " 'The Curse of Eden Eld,' " Otto read in an ominous tone.

"A curse?" Eleanor whispered. Her fingertips were cold. Frozen cold. Her whole hands, too. She curled her fingers, trying to keep them warm by making fists. *It's cursed, that place. I've tried to keep you safe. But I can't anymore. I'm sorry. I'm sorry,* her mother's voice said in her memory. "What kind of curse?"

"It says—hold on," Otto said, turning the magazine back around as Pip and Eleanor clustered close. " 'A sleepy town called Eden Eld is said to harbor a terrible secret. Every thirteen years, on Halloween night, three children go missing.' " Otto gulped, but pressed on. " 'None of them have ever been found.' "

"That can't be true," Pip objected. "We would have heard about it. There would be news stories."

"I'm just telling you what it says," Otto said, exasperated, and pushed the magazine toward them. "Read it yourself."

Part of the page was taken up with a clearly photoshopped picture of a forest with a full moon shining between the trees. Otto had skipped past the headline, but it was obvious that the article was about scary stories from different places. The first one on the page was about someplace called Briar Glen in Massachusetts, and the last one just had the header and a couple sentences about a town in Florida, but the one in the middle was for Eden Eld. After the one-line introduction, the article continued.

> Eden Eld is a small town in a mostly forgotten part of Oregon. There is not much to see there—a private school of some repute, towering pines that keep the town's logging industry running, and a mine off in the hills that has long since shuttered. But even Eden Eld has its ghost stories—and they are stranger and wilder than most.
>
> The town is haunted by a peculiar trio of spirits—ghosts, monsters, apparitions, you tell me. They're seen from time to time, but most especially on Halloween. They are called the People Who Look Away, and chief among them

is the figure known as the Backward-Facing Man—or, to some, Mr. January. He is tall and thin, and when he is sighted at a distance, he is always facing away from you, for he only shows his face to those he means to trick. And what a trickster he is.

It is said that Mr. January was there when Eden Eld was founded, and that he struck a deal with the town's first residents. He would make sure their town thrived, but in return, every thirteen years he would take three of their children. Not just any children—these children were marked, because they were born on *his* day. Halloween. Thirteen times he would do this, and then the deal would be fulfilled.

The settlers, who had crossed a continent to claim this land, and who had suffered and lost along the way, reluctantly agreed. They set about making their town. Thirteen years later, it was formally established, and three accidental deaths were recorded. Three children, aged thirteen exactly, swept away in a mysterious flood. No bodies were ever recovered.

Thirteen years later, no such deaths were reported. Journals and records, along with those few stories older locals are willing to whisper, suggest that the town simply stopped talking about the People Who Look Away and Mr. January. They treated the marked children distantly, and when the children disappeared, they pretended it had not happened at all.

In time, that pretending grew and turned malignant, like a cancer. By the fifth such Halloween, it wasn't just that the townsfolk chose not to see—they couldn't see. They forgot. They made up stories. They recorded accidental deaths on other days, put the wrong dates on birth certificates, or simply seemed to . . . not notice. And so if you ask someone in Eden Eld why so many children disappear, they will tell you, without a hint of deception, that children don't disappear in Eden Eld.

They are not lying. But they are not telling the truth.

If you visit Eden Eld, beware of anyone who won't turn toward you. And if a sly stranger offers you a deal, here's some advice: check his footprints. Because even when you think you see his face, the footprints of the People Who Look Away are turned the wrong way around. And any deal they offer isn't one you want to take.

And remember the numbers—31313.

That's how you'll see the truth.

Twelve

Eleanor looked up from the magazine. "It's the same as the fairy tale. I mean—almost."

"Did you read the whole thing already?" Pip asked, eyebrows raised.

"Yes?" Eleanor said.

"Seriously? You read fast," Pip said, scrunching up her nose in a way that suggested *she* didn't read very fast at all, and felt a bit bad about it. She turned her attention back to the article, frowning at the page for another minute before she looked up. "Then we aren't the first," she said.

"Whatever's happening to us, it's happened to other kids before," Eleanor agreed. "Lots of them. And people just . . . forgot."

"Like they forget about the wrong things," Otto added.

You can see. You can see what others can't, as long as you look. It won't keep you safe, but it'll keep you smart, her mother had said. Not that last night, that horrible night, but before. When things were only just starting to get bad.

"The January Society is descended from the founders. They're keeping up the deal with Mr. January," Eleanor said slowly. Something was bothering her again, itching at the back of her brain. Something about silver cufflinks. "And what's with these numbers? They were underlined in the book, too. Three, thirteen, thirteen."

"There are thirteen stories in the book," Pip said. "And we're thirteen. And there are three of us."

It's all thirteens. The first part of what her mother said in the dream last night had really happened—she'd made Eleanor promise so many times not to go back to Eden Eld. But thirteens? She'd never said anything about that. Not that Eleanor could remember. But she'd said a lot of strange things near the end. Eleanor had started blocking them out.

"So three thirteens. Maybe that's about us," Pip said.

"What else does the magazine say?" Otto asked. Pip flipped forward and back, but the article didn't have anything more about Eden Eld.

"Hold on," Eleanor said, stabbing her finger against the previous page. "Look who wrote it!"

The article was by *Professor Andrew Ashford.*

"Andy Ashford," Eleanor said. "He owned the book. He must have been the one who underlined the numbers. They *have* to mean something." Then she gasped. "Wait! I've seen them before. They're on the Founders' Monument!" She fished around in her backpack. She still had the worksheet from history class in there, with the first answer written in her small, neat handwriting.

Eden Eld

Founded 1851

Drawn Onward

31313

"Three, thirteen, thirteen," Otto said triumphantly.

"Three turn thirteen every thirteen years," Eleanor said. "Just like the story said."

"Or . . ." Otto made light slashes between the numbers with his finger. Not 3-13-13, but 31-3-13. "On the thirty-first, three turn thirteen. It works either way."

It works either way. Something itched at Eleanor, but she still couldn't figure out why. She chewed on the edge of her lip.

She'd read every story at least three times, even the ones that didn't seem to have anything to do with Eden Eld. Little things jumped out at her, but she didn't know if they were important. The Orchard Thieves put leaves in the poet's mouth to keep him from talking. Jack never went anywhere without his walking stick. The girl with backward hands carried the rose Jack had stolen from the Cerulean King's garden, its petals growing back whenever she plucked them.

They wove in and out of one another, the stories. The rattle-bird was in more than one and Jack was the hero of "Tatterskin" and "The Brackenbeast," and a character called the hedgewitch brought a present to the Glass-Heart Girl, and then made the magic slippers in "The Girl Who Danced with the Moon." The girl with her hands turned backward showed up with Jack and the hedgewitch a lot, like they were friends, though it never explained how they'd met. The stories all braided together, looping and twining and making complicated knots that Eleanor couldn't see how to undo.

But the People Who Look Away were in almost all of the stories. Sometimes they were just in the background. Sometimes they were even helpful—for a certain definition of helpful that usually led to a different kind of trouble than the heroes started with. But a lot of the time they were the reason that things went wrong.

In "Jack and the Hungry House," the man from the first story was the one who convinced Jack's mother that he needed to go and earn his fortune. At the end, when Jack came home and found his mother gone and the man in the house, he asked the man who he was. Eleanor couldn't remember exactly what the man said, so she took out the book and opened it on her lap where she sat cross-legged on the floor.

I am no one and I am everyone, the man said. *Whichever way you look at me, I'm looking back at you. Or am I looking away, even when we're face-to-face? I am the end and the beginning, the forward and the back.* She stopped and read it again, silently. "Huh," she said.

"What is it? Did you figure something out?" Pip asked.

"It just sounds like he's talking about a palindrome," Eleanor said.

"What's that?" Pip asked.

"It's a word or a sentence that's the same forward and backward," Eleanor explained. "Like the number. 31313. It's the same whichever way you read it."

"It's symmetrical," Otto said. "When something is the same end to end, it's got bilateral symmetry. Like a human body. One arm and leg on each side, one eye on each side and everything. My name's symmetrical, too."

"That makes it a palindrome," Eleanor said, nodding. Something clicked into place. "Janus!" she said.

"The god?" Pip asked. At Otto's confused look, she explained. "He's from Greek mythology. He's the god of beginnings and endings. Like January, because it's the end of one year and the beginning of the other. Oh, also, he has two faces, one in each direction."

"Your mom was wearing Janus cufflinks," Eleanor said.

"My dad bought those for her," Pip said. "I thought it was just because he likes Greek myths. He bought me this big book of them, and . . ." She trailed off. Otto squeezed her shoulder, a comforting gesture.

"A man that faces forward and back at the same time. That sounds a lot like the People Who Look Away," Otto said.

"It's like how the fairy tales are a sneaky way of talking about what's really happening," Eleanor said. "Because you can't say it outright. You need a story to hide it. So they use Janus, but they're *really* talking about *him*. It's probably why they call him Mr. January. Janus is where the name January comes from."

"Wait. Pip is a palindrome, too, isn't it?" Otto asked.

"But not Philippa," Pip said.

"Even your parents have always called you Pip, though," Otto said.

"Well, Eleanor's not a palindrome. Rona-el-e," Pip sounded out. "So maybe it doesn't mean anything."

Eleanor drew in a sharp little breath. Her hands were getting cold again. She pressed them against the pages of the book, but it didn't offer any warmth. "I decided to go by Eleanor when I moved here," she said. "But I never have before. My mom always called me—"

"Elle," Otto finished for her. She met his eyes and nodded once.

"Our birthdays are one thing," Eleanor said. "You don't *really* control what day you have a baby on, or when you get pregnant. But our names? If our names are part of this—"

"Our parents picked our names," Pip said, realization dawning.

"You remember the story. The children were marked as his," Eleanor said. "What if it didn't just mean that they had the right birthday? What if people gave them special names so that you knew right away you weren't—weren't supposed to get attached? '*Marked in flesh and name.*' That's what the poem said."

"That would mean it wasn't just my parents, though," Pip said. "I mean—I knew my mom was a bad person. She says all the right nice things and she makes casseroles when people are sick and donates to charity, but she's just *bad* inside. She doesn't love me. She looks at me and she doesn't love me and I've always known that. My dad's okay, except he's got to be evil, too, since he's in the January Society. So maybe he doesn't love me, either. Not really. But this means Otto's parents—your parents—" Pip's face was a tangle of different emotions. Like she was horrified and hopeful at the same time at the idea that she wasn't the only one with a wicked family.

"My parents *do* love me," Otto shot back. "And if they knew I was going to get sacrificed or whatever, they'd try to protect me. They wouldn't stay here, for one thing. And I bet Eleanor's parents weren't evil, either. I bet they didn't know any more than mine do."

Eleanor swallowed. She was pressing her hands so hard against the book she was suddenly afraid she would damage it. She pulled them away and made fists with them instead. "My mom knew," she said.

Otto looked startled. "What?"

"I lied. My parents didn't die in a car crash. They aren't dead at all. Or they might be. I don't know. I don't even know who my dad is. My mom—" She took a deep breath. Her thumb traced the crescent scar on her palm. "My mom moved away from Eden Eld right after she had me. My grandparents always tried to get her to come back, but she wouldn't. And she made me promise I would never come here, either. She was always kind of . . . strange. But a few months ago, she started to get more and more scared. Saying strange things. She'd get up ten times in the night to check that all the doors and windows were locked, and she stopped letting me go to school. And then one day she lit our house on fire and disappeared."

"Whoa," Pip said. She wrapped her arms around her body, her fingers picking at the folds of her shirt with nervous energy.

"She was trying to protect you," Otto said.

"And then she tried to kill me," Eleanor shot back. "So I guess she was evil after all. And maybe your parents—"

"No," Otto said, shaking his head. "There's some other explanation, because my parents love me, and they're the most normal people in the world. My mom's a children's librarian, and she won't even kill spiders. My dad is a vet. He nurses tiny baby kittens with his own hands. He could charge way higher prices, but he treats tons of his patients for free because they can't pay and he doesn't want to turn anyone away. There's no *way* they're evil."

"But you *are* descended from one of the founding families," Pip insisted. "And you have the right kind of name."

"So maybe someone suggested it to them," Eleanor cut in quickly, because she could see that Otto was getting ready to really argue and she didn't want them fighting.

"What I don't get is why you'd hide all this in a book of fairy tales," Pip said. "If somebody wanted to tell you how to fight the wrong things, why not just make a textbook or something?"

Eleanor thought. And then she spoke slowly. "It's like you said, with trying to show people the wrong things. Sometimes, it's hard to see the truth when it's right in front of you," she said. "Sometimes you can only see it if you look at it out of the corner of your eye. Or if you tell a story about it. If people don't notice or don't remember the things that happen here, you couldn't exactly warn them about it. But maybe if you put them into stories, stories that didn't seem to be about Eden Eld at all but which told you how to protect yourself . . ."

"Like sprinkling the flour at the wedding," Otto said.

"And that crystal the king's sister is holding in the illustration," Eleanor said. "It's not in the story, but it's in the picture. I bet that's important."

"So it's like . . . a guide. Just a sneaky one," Pip said.

"Right. So even if your mind was all wired to ignore the wrong things, it could remember the stories."

"Will it tell us how to save ourselves?" Pip asked, shifting from side to side.

"I don't know," Eleanor said. "But I trust books. And I think we can trust this one. Besides, we don't really have any other ideas."

She waited for one of them to chime in to tell her they didn't need the book, that they knew a way to save themselves, that it would all be okay. But both of them looked grim.

"I don't know what to do," Pip said softly.

"We know one thing for sure," Eleanor said, forcing every bit of iron she had into her voice. "We have to get out of Eden Eld. And we have to do it today."

Thirteen

They couldn't leave right away. If they missed their classes, people would come looking for them. Besides, they'd need to get supplies if they were going to get far enough away. How far that was, they didn't know.

"We'll meet up at Ashford House after school," Pip declared. "It's right on the border of town, so it's the best place to start from. We'll head through the woods. We just need to find somewhere to hide long enough to wait out Halloween."

They all agreed. It seemed foolproof. Something bad was coming for Eden Eld on Halloween—so leave Eden Eld. Simple.

So Eleanor kept telling herself as she sat through the rest of her classes. So she told herself on the bus ride home, sitting next to the uncharacteristically silent Otto. At his stop he got up, then hesitated, his backpack slung over one shoulder.

"This is going to work, isn't it?" he asked. "We'll be safe?"

"It'll work," she told him. "I'm sure of it."

Lying got so very easy after a while.

He hopped off the bus. She watched him make his way down a long gravel driveway, vanishing among the trees. She'd see him again soon, she told herself, but she couldn't bring herself to think what might happen after that.

Jenny was napping when she got home, so she went through the kitchen cupboards, finding enough food to last a couple days and stowing it in her backpack. Warm clothes were next, and then she found herself frozen in the middle of her room, trying to think of what to bring, terrified that she'd forget the one thing that might save them.

She grabbed the book and sat down on her bed, tucking her feet under her. She turned the pages, as if an answer would jump out at her. She wished she were as brave as Jack, the hero in so many of the stories, or as clever as the girl with backward hands who went on several of his adventures with him. And then there was the hedgewitch, too, who always seemed to have a magical brew or a pair of charmed boots to save the day—and who, it had to be said, seemed to have something going on with Jack, though the stories never came out and said it.

She didn't have a magic walking stick like Jack, or a satchel of potions like the hedgewitch, or an enchanted rose like the girl with backward hands. But there were three of them, and she and Pip and Otto made three, and maybe that was enough. Maybe *they* were enough.

She flipped through to the end of the book to a number of

blank pages where the thirteenth story ought to have been. The first of the blank pages had smudges on it—no, the ghosts of words she still couldn't quite read. She squinted at the title.

The Thirt—

It was all she could make out.

Clack!

Something sharp hit the window, and Eleanor jumped. Then another one hit. *Clack!* A rock. Being thrown from down below.

"Pip," Eleanor said with relief, and ran to the window. Pip and Otto stood below, their bikes beside them and their backpacks stuffed full. Pip waved wildly. Eleanor waved back and held up a "wait a minute" finger. She stuffed the book in her bag and ran for the stairs.

Her path brought her past the kitchen. Jenny was up, sipping a glass of water between blowing out long, tense breaths. "Hey, Elle," she said. "Where are you off to?"

Guilt jabbed Eleanor between her ribs. One more lie, she thought, and then she wouldn't lie to Jenny and Ben ever again. "Just going out to explore a bit with Pip and Otto," she said. "I'll be back for dinner."

"Have fun," Jenny said, obviously distracted by the state of her belly.

Eleanor slunk away. She headed down the steps and around the side of the house, where Pip and Otto were waiting.

"There you are," Pip said, as if she'd taken five hours and not five minutes. "Ready to go?"

Eleanor nodded.

"We'll stow the bikes in the trees. They're no good in the forest," Pip said. "But it was the fastest way to get here."

Otto shivered. Nerves, or the cold? Eleanor decided not to ask. "Do you know where we're going?" she asked.

"Yeah, kinda," Pip said. She pointed with her whole hand, away from the house and the road. "Out past the old orchard, the forest is super thick. I looked at some old maps, and it's not really obvious where exactly Eden Eld stops, but we're definitely near the edge of it now. So we shouldn't have to go too far to get out. If we keep walking until after dark, we should be able to get a couple miles past the border. And tomorrow we can keep going. The next town is only six miles away, so we should be able to reach it tomorrow. Then we just wait until November first and call home for a ride."

Aunt Jenny and Uncle Ben would be worried, but there was no way to avoid that. "Let's go," Eleanor said.

They started out across the orchard. The trees were all apple trees, but only a few scattered fruits grew, tiny and wizened, with hardly any color in their skins. Ben kept saying he was going to find out how to nurse the orchard back to health—in all his free time. Then he'd laugh, and then he'd sigh.

The branches seemed to clatter as they passed, though there wasn't any wind. They picked up the pace, and soon they'd reached the end of the apple trees and the beginning of the pines, where the shadows stitched together into a solid tapestry of black. There they slowed, and Eleanor pretended it was because it was hard to see in the dim light and navigate the treacherous tree roots, and not that they were afraid.

The pines blocked out the sky, except for ragged, pale scraps here and there. In the dark underforest, nothing moved except the three of them, and the thick carpet of pine needles hushed their footsteps into silence.

"Straight on," Pip muttered, but Eleanor wasn't sure who she was talking to. "Straight on."

Something rattled in the trees. Pip gasped and stumbled. Eleanor grabbed her hand to steady her, and they held each other and their breath, waiting for the sound to come again.

"Just wind," Otto offered, but then it came again. *Clackclack-clack*. Moving closer and closer.

"Run!" Pip hiss-whispered, and they bolted farther into the forest. Eleanor's bag slapped hard against her back. Roots grabbed at her feet, and it seemed like she'd barely gone three steps before she was panting for breath through a tight, cold chest. Pip was the fastest of them, but she wouldn't go too far ahead, bouncing nervously when she had to slow to keep pace.

Clackclackclack. Clackclackclack. A harsh croak chased after the sounds, and a gurgle almost like laughter. Eleanor dared a glance behind them. It came through the trees, huge wings made of shadow, swooping from branch to branch. Its eyes gleamed an oily yellow-orange. *Clackclackclack. Clackclackclack.* "Look out!" Otto yelled, and grabbed Eleanor by the shoulder, stopping her up short so hard they almost fell over together.

A dark form rose from the forest floor, eyes opening, glowing red. The graveyard dog. It growled, pacing toward them.

"This way!" Pip called, and they ran to the left. The dog barked and bounded, chasing after them.

There was no way they were faster than the dog, Eleanor thought wildly, and expected at any moment for its teeth to clamp shut around her leg. It snarled and snapped behind them, never drawing closer, but always keeping pace. And then Eleanor realized—it was herding them. Driving them back the way they had come.

Figures flapped and screeched and rattled from the shadows, forcing them to turn, and turn again, until Eleanor had no idea where they were going. The light was fading, and she couldn't see the direction of the sun.

And then—they stumbled out. Out of the trees. They'd emerged near the road, in front of Ashford House.

"No," Pip cried. Sickening dread shuddered through Eleanor.

A car crouched in the driveway, sleek and red as a poisoned apple. Ms. Foster stood beside the driver's side door, her hands folded in front of her, looking right at them.

The snarling and rattling behind them fell silent. Eleanor looked back. Yellow-orange and smoldering red, the beasts' eyes were all she could make out from the edge of the wood. But they were watching. Waiting. There was no escaping Eden Eld.

Even from this distance, she could see Ms. Foster's brilliant smile.

Fourteen

Eleanor was silent through dinner. She could barely eat.

Pip and Otto had gone home with Ms. Foster. There'd been no point in running, not with the beasts behind them and Ms. Foster right there. They'd traded quick whispers, cobbling together a plan in the steps between the trees and the driveway. They'd just have to sneak out again tonight. They might not be able to get away from Eden Eld altogether, but if they could stay away from the January Society, it might be enough.

They just had to wait until the adults were asleep.

Eleanor watched the glowing numbers on the microwave and ran her fingers over the scar on her palm. Not long now. Not long at all.

"We should do something for your birthday," Jenny said suddenly. Her contractions had taken a break long enough for her to eat in comfort, and she seemed buoyed by the brief respite. "We've been so busy we haven't set anything up. I feel terrible. Maybe we could have some of your friends over? Pip and Otto?"

Eleanor stared at her. She felt numb. Like she couldn't feel *anything*. "That would be nice," she said dully.

Ben's brow furrowed. "You okay there, sport?"

"I don't feel very well," Eleanor said. At least that wasn't a lie. But she wouldn't be able to sit here much longer without lying about *something*.

There might be a curse ready to snatch her away come midnight, but she was suddenly angry most of all that it had taken Ben and Jenny from her. She couldn't tell them the truth. They couldn't help her. She had lost her mother and she was losing them, too, even though they were right in front of her.

"Is it okay if I just go to bed?" she asked. She would look in the book again. If she read it one more time, maybe she would see the solution, the way to save them all and stop the curse from taking them.

"Of course," Jenny said. "Do you need us to bring you anything? Cocoa? Tea?"

Eleanor just shook her head. She hurried out, feeling their eyes on her, wishing they could help her, wishing she could reassure them. In her room she climbed into her bed and tucked herself against the pillows, bending over the book.

Something scraped outside her window.

She sat bolt upright. *Just a branch,* she thought, but there were no trees that close to this side of the house that were anywhere near tall enough to reach the third floor. She pulled herself back against the headboard.

There was something crouched on her windowsill—something big and black, with two bright green eyes that stared in at her, unblinking. And then it stood, and she saw its shape properly. It was a cat. An enormous cat, with thick, long fur.

The cat stood up on its hind legs, putting its big front paws on the glass of the window—and then it slid right through. It jumped, smooth and graceful, and thumped lightly onto the floor. It shook itself a little, sending gray flecks flying in all directions. And then, with a single leap, it sprang up onto the end of her bed and sat there, twitching its tail and staring at her.

"I know what you are," Eleanor said. She meant to say it in a strong voice, but it came out a whisper.

"Is that so?" asked the cat, its voice feminine, silky and deep. Its mouth did not move, but Eleanor heard the voice plain and clear. "Then who am I, pet?"

"You're the cat-of-ashes," Eleanor said.

"So I am," the cat said. "Good. You're a few steps ahead of the last bunch, then. You're clever, I can tell. And sharp. Two of my favorite things to be. But clever enough? Sharp enough? Hm." She flicked her tail across the bedspread, leaving a streak of ash. She smelled of burnt things, like woodsmoke and charcoal.

"The last bunch? What last bunch?"

"Oh dear. Not so far ahead as I'd hoped," the cat said. The cat stood and took several steps toward her. Her weight pulled the blankets tighter over Eleanor's legs. She stopped with one paw lifted as Eleanor pressed farther against the headboard. "Frightened, are you? You needn't be. No one can touch you, except on All Hallows' Eve. Midnight to midnight. And it's just now—"

The clock in the hall chimed the hour.

Eight.

The cat's ear swiveled toward the noise, then back again. "A little time left before the games begin."

"What games?" Eleanor whispered.

"That depends on you. Some years it's not sporting at all," the cat said. "And sometimes it's a near thing indeed. The teams are a bit stacked, of course, and only one side has won so far, but that could always change. Personally, I root for you kids every time. I'm a sucker for the underdog story." She laughed, low and throaty, and blinked her big green eyes. "They're going to come for you, little beast, and put you through the door to the gray, and then you'll belong to him, and to his sisters. That's the way it works. That's the deal that's been struck. Unless you can wiggle your way out of it, which I'm rather hoping you can."

"But you work for them. For him. Mr. January." Eleanor said the name with confidence she didn't feel, but the cat-of-ashes didn't contradict her.

"Cats do not *work*," she said with disdain. "But I will allow that my activities do serve him. I hate the man, but I haven't much of a choice in it, I'm afraid. Still, I can sneak in a little rebellion here and there. I wouldn't be able to call myself *cat* if I couldn't."

"Are you his prisoner?" Eleanor asked. "Could we free you? Could—"

"Now, now. That won't get you anywhere. My troubles can't be solved quick enough to do you any good, and even if you broke my bonds, dear, I'm a cat. We aren't known for our constancy. I'd probably wander off and forget to help."

Eleanor couldn't tell if the cat was making fun of her, but she was less and less afraid. Of the cat, at least. "You said they're coming for us. Who?"

"Oh, dear. If you can't figure *that* out, you're doomed for sure."

"But *someone* is coming for us. Me and Otto and Pip."

"That's right, little beast," the cat said. "You're the mice in this trap, and it's closing fast."

"Can you help us now? You must know how we can save ourselves. Even just a little hint."

"There are things I can't say, and things I shouldn't say, and things I don't care to say," the cat said. "But personally, I have never liked *shouldn't*. I'll give you this much, and then you're on your own. Bartimaeus Ashford has an ego bigger than the house he built to satisfy it, and he is *almost* as clever as he believes he is. This place is still full of his tricks, if you know where to look, and some of them might come in handy."

"Where?" Eleanor asked.

"Tsk-tsk. If you need me to tell you everything, I don't see how you have any chance of surviving," the cat-of-ashes said. She stretched, nails raking the bedspread and leaving scorch marks. "I already brought you the book, and that's more than any of the others got. But because your mother is such a nice woman and always scratches that spot behind my ear, I'll tell you one more thing: everything in this house has a purpose. Everything."

With that, she jumped down onto the floor.

"Wait! You know my mom? Where is she?" Eleanor demanded, flinging off the covers and leaping onto the floor herself. But the cat-of-ashes was already bounding to the windowsill. She paused on this side of the glass and lashed her tail one last time.

"*That* I can't tell you, but I'm sure you'll find out on your own. Now remember, little beast. Between midnight and midnight, you're vulnerable. And the next time we see each other, you'd do well to be afraid."

"If you can't tell me where my mother is, can you tell me why she tried to kill me?" Eleanor demanded.

The cat's eyes widened. "Now, who told you a thing like *that*?" she asked. Her tail thrashed. Then the cat-of-ashes leaped from the windowsill and out of sight.

Eleanor lurched after her, running to the window, but there was no sign of the cat. Eleanor's heart beat hard in her chest. Of course her mother had set the fire. There was no one else in the house to do it.

Was there?

Eleanor ran her thumb along the shiny part of her palm, the scar the scalding doorknob had left. Why would she warn

Eleanor to stay away from Eden Eld right before she lit the house on fire?

What if she hadn't set it? What if she hadn't run away?

What if she had been taken?

The thought was heavy as a stone, and it dragged Eleanor down to the floor in a crouch. She wrapped her arms around her knees. What if her mother wasn't evil, and she needed Eleanor's help?

She wanted to run out and find her right away, but she had no idea where to go—and she couldn't leave Eden Eld. And even if she managed that, she couldn't save her mother—if she really needed saving—until she'd saved herself. And Pip. And Otto.

Midnight to midnight. They had less than four hours left. She listened to the ticking of the clock, and she waited.

Fifteen

At ten forty-five, thirty minutes after Ben and Jenny had gone to bed, Eleanor shoved the book into her backpack. She held her shoes in one hand and hurried down the steps in her socks so she'd be quiet, and even managed to dodge the creakiest floorboards. When she was almost at the back door, she stopped and backtracked. She ducked into the living room, where the giant fireplace stood, the staircase leading into shadows at the back of it. A heavy set of iron fire tools sat next to the fireplace, untouched for years. The kids in "The Graveyard Dog" had used an iron shovel to drive the dog off. Hopefully an iron fire poker would do just as well.

She stuck it into her backpack, closing the zipper around it to hold it in place, and ran to the back door.

There was no bus to take her to Otto's. She couldn't run that far, and even if she knew how to drive, she thought stealing Ben and Jenny's car would *probably* wake them up. But she'd seen some old bikes in the shed, so she sprinted across the scrubby grass, ignoring just how spooky the orchard looked at night.

She pulled open the door. It groaned and whined but gave. The old car was under a cloth to keep the dust off. The bicycles shoved against the wall next to it didn't get the same protection, and they were practically one big cobweb. Eleanor picked the smaller of the two and wheeled it out. It wobbled a little, and the wheel made a whine of its own, but she didn't have time to oil it. She did her best to swipe the dust off the handlebars and the seat, then flung her leg over.

The pedals were stiff at first, and as she worked her way up the dirt track to the road, she thought she would have gone faster at a brisk walk. But they loosened up as she pedaled, and the effort kept her warm even though she'd forgotten a coat. Soon she was sailing down the road in the dark.

The wind bit at her, but it was worth it for the speed. She pedaled as fast as she could, her legs already aching. She had to get to the others. It was all she thought about. Her plan, her list: Get to Pip. Get to Otto. Stay safe. Stay free. Find the answer.

She was wheezing for breath by the time she saw the lights at the end of Otto's drive—and the black car parked just down the road, its lights off but a figure in the driver's seat. She wrenched the bike to the side, careening off the road before they could spot her, and pulled herself and the bike behind a big pine. She peered around the trunk, hoping she hadn't been seen. The car didn't move. Neither did the person in it. From the way their head was tipped down, she thought they might be asleep.

Mr. January? Did Mr. January drive a car? No—it had to be someone from the January Society. She couldn't make out the person's features, or even if it was a man or a woman, and she didn't want to stick around to find out. She couldn't ride the bike through the trees, so she walked it beside her, staying low over the handlebars in the hopes that she wouldn't be spotted.

She didn't really know where she was going, but the old truck where they'd agreed to meet up was easy to find even in the dark, a white beacon. It was weird—she'd seen plenty of abandoned cars and trucks before, but never one that looked so perfect. There wasn't a single chip in the paint or crack in the windshield, and the tires looked in pristine condition. She'd have thought the truck was brand-new if it wasn't old-fashioned—and if a tree hadn't begun to grow around the back bumper.

"Hey," Otto whispered, stepping out from behind the truck. "You made it." He bounced from foot to foot with nervous energy.

"There's someone in a car by your driveway," she said.

"I know. He's been there for like an hour," Otto replied.

"What's with the truck?" she asked.

"Huh?" Otto looked confused.

"How does it look so good?"

He shrugged. "I don't know. It's been there all my life."

"So shouldn't it be all rusted and stuff?"

"I guess, but—"

"Things don't rust in Eden Eld," Eleanor guessed. He nodded. "It's the deal. Everything is so perfect because of the deal. And no one thinks it's strange, for the same reason they don't notice the wrong things."

"I guess that explains why I never have to mow the lawn," Otto said. Otto's phone chirped in his pocket.

"Turn that on silent!" Eleanor chided as he pulled it out.

"Sorry. It's Pip." He showed her the screen and the text displayed on it.

SOS JAN AT HOUSE

JAN had to mean January Society. "They're at her house," Eleanor said. "Or she's stuck at the house?"

"Either way, we have to go get her," Otto said, data and caution thrown aside with his friend in danger.

"We can't take the roads if the Society's out. They might see us," Eleanor said.

"There's a back way. A path through the woods. It's a bit rough, but the bikes should be okay."

There was no time to waste. They set off on their bikes, bumping over the uneven ground.

The dorms for resident students were on the other side of the athletic fields, but Pip stayed in her family's house, and *that* was a little farther away. Down a road through the trees, tucked just out of sight.

When they were still a little ways out, they hid the bikes and crept forward on foot, staying well away from the road.

The ground-floor lights were on, but the curtains were closed. There was a small gap where the light leaked through, and Eleanor pointed at it. "I'm going to go get a look inside," she whispered.

"Careful," Otto urged her.

Careful had gone out the window when she'd left Ashford House, she thought, but she stayed low and slow as she approached. She crept up to the flowerbeds out front—packed with the purple flowers, so thick she could barely find a clear place to step—and listened. There were voices inside. Ms. Foster and someone else—Mr. Foster, she assumed.

"Seventeen minutes," Ms. Foster said.

"You can't make time pass faster by checking your watch," Mr. Foster replied.

A sigh and the click of heels across the floor as Ms. Foster paced. "I just want to get this over with. The others are in position?"

"Or close to it. It needn't be on the hour, Delilah. The children are asleep. Philippa is locked in her room. Twelve oh one or twelve fifteen won't matter very much." He sounded a bit exasperated.

"And Jennifer Barton and that big lunk she married won't be a problem? She's having contractions. She won't be sleeping well."

"It's a big house, and the girl is on the third floor. I'm sure the team can handle the extraction," he replied.

Eleanor sucked in a sharp breath between her clenched teeth. Pip was right, then. Her parents *were* evil. But at least Ben and Jenny didn't know. She hoped Pip's father was right, and they wouldn't wake up. They'd be safe, as long as they stayed asleep.

She crept back to Otto and relayed what she'd heard. He looked queasy. "I gave her such a hard time," he said. "I never really believed her. I thought her mom was just *mean*. Who would sacrifice their own daughter?"

Eleanor didn't have an answer for him. "Where's Pip's bedroom?" she asked instead.

"This way."

They crept around the side of the house. The bedrooms were on the second floor. Eleanor peered up. There were three windows, and she could tell which one was Pip's without Otto's help. The one on the far left had sports trophies lined up on the windowsill. Soccer, field hockey, horseback riding. A trellis covered in vines, withered with the fall, stood against the wall beside it. Eleanor tried it. She didn't weigh much. It would probably hold her. Or it would break and dump her on the ground and make a ton of noise, but they didn't have time for caution.

"I'll go up. You keep a lookout," Eleanor said. Otto nodded. Between the two of them, she was marginally more athletic, but that wasn't saying much. They really could have used Pip right now. But then they wouldn't need to be rescuing Pip, she supposed.

She hauled herself up one step at a time until she could lean out and knock on the window.

Nothing. She knocked again.

Pip's face appeared in the window, pale and confused. When she saw Eleanor, her eyes widened. Eleanor gestured frantically. Pip opened the window a crack. "You came! Where's Otto?" she whispered. "Is he okay?"

"He's right below us," Eleanor replied. "I heard your parents talking. You're locked in?" She wobbled on the trellis.

"And they took my phone. I managed to delete the text first, at least," Pip said.

"We've got to get you out of here."

"The window doesn't open any wider. It's stuck," Pip said.

Eleanor peered at it. There were nails driven into the frame, blocking the window from opening more than a couple inches. They'd been painted over a few times—they must have been there for years. Eleanor shivered, and not from the cold. The Fosters had been planning this a long time. "If I can get these nails out, maybe we can get the window open," she said.

"Nails? Hold on," Pip said. She ducked back inside. Eleanor leaned farther to watch. Pip's room was a mess, covered in clothes and half-finished art projects. Pip stuffed some things into her backpack hastily. Stairs creaked somewhere deeper in the house, and she wrenched the zipper shut, then grabbed something from a drawer. She handed it through the gap. Pliers.

"Jewelry-making phase," she explained.

It took several minutes of prying and pulling and it left her fingers cramping, but Eleanor managed to prize both of the nails out. The window was stiff, and it took both of them to force it up, but it opened all the way. Eleanor scrambled back down the trellis.

With her backpack over her shoulder, Pip flung herself over the windowsill, balanced for one moment with her feet dangling, and then kicked out and dropped.

She landed with a grunt and a thump, but the soft dirt absorbed most of the noise. She crouched beside Eleanor, panting a little, and she and Otto gave each other a hasty high five.

"I knew you guys would come for me," Pip said. "How'd you get here?"

"Bikes," Otto answered.

Pip nodded. "Mine's by the garage. Hurry!"

They scuttled along the back of the house and darted across the grass to the garage, which stood apart from the rest of the house. In the gap between rested a shiny blue bike. It looked expensive. More importantly, it looked fast.

A light went on upstairs in the house. And then Ms. Foster shouted, the words indistinct but the tone furious.

"Run!" Pip said, but Eleanor grabbed her arm.

"No! Slow. Sneaky," she said. She pulled Pip around the side of the house, Otto following close behind, and into the woods, deeper in the shadows where they couldn't be seen from the house. Pip and Otto walked the bike between them, staying crouched as low as possible, as all the rest of the lights went on one by one.

They'd reached the spot where Eleanor and Otto had stashed their bicycles when an engine roared to life. They froze. They dropped to the ground at the same time. Eleanor grabbed Pip's dark blue backpack and yanked it up to cover her bright red hair, then pressed her own face to the ground as the headlights of the car reached them. The car rolled forward slowly, like whoever was driving was searching the trees. Eleanor counted her breaths instead and forced herself to keep them slow.

Finally, the lights swept past them. Eleanor kept her head down until the sound of the engine faded. Then she sat up gingerly.

"They didn't see us," Otto said.

"I think we're in the clear for now," Eleanor agreed. Pip nodded. Her cheek was smeared with dirt, and there were tear-tracks running through it. "Are you okay?"

"I was hoping I was wrong," Pip said, and burst into tears.

Eleanor wrapped her arms around Pip, and Otto did the same from the other side. Pip put her head on Eleanor's shoulder and cried great hiccupping sobs that shook her whole body. Eleanor just made soothing noises and patted her back, meeting Otto's eyes and feeling as helpless as Jenny and Ben must have felt all the time since they took her in. "Hey," she said. "Hey, now." You couldn't hold in sadness like that. It made you sick. But Eleanor only cried when no one could see.

She was glad that Pip, at least, wasn't alone.

Pip straightened up, scrubbing at her runny nose. Even in the dark Eleanor could see her splotchy cheeks. Pip gulped down a breath of air and shoved her hair back behind her ears. It tangled in a scraggly mess around her face, but that suited

Pip. "Aren't you going to say everything's going to be okay, or something?" Pip asked.

"No," Eleanor said. "People say that a lot to me and it never helps. It just makes me mad. Because everything isn't okay. Even if it turns out better in the end, it'll never be okay that this happened."

"I just didn't say anything because I have no idea what to say," Otto confessed.

"That's a first," Pip said, and bumped her shoulder against his. He bumped her back. Pip took a deep breath. "Enough crying. Let's get going," she declared, and got to her feet.

Otto's phone chimed. "Uh-oh," he said "That's the alarm. One minute to midnight."

The air grew colder around them. The wind stirred through the trees. And Eleanor heard it: the *tick tock tick* of a clock. *The* clock, though they were miles away, though it was tucked inside the halls of Ashford House.

Thirty seconds. The wind howled, sending leaves scattering furiously around them, whipping at their hair and their clothes. Otto yelped in alarm. And then—everything went still. The wind ceased. The branches stopped their creaking. The leaves settled.

Ten seconds. There was only their breathing and that steady *tick tock tick tock . . .*

Tick . . .

Tock.

And then the chiming of the clock. One. Two. Three. Eleanor whispered, counting each of them out. Nine. Ten. Eleven.

Twelve.

A soft wind sighed through the trees, setting everything shivering. And the color went out of the world.

It happened slowly at first, and then in a rush, with Pip's hair losing its coppery shine, Otto's blue jacket sinking into dull gray, even the light of the phone in his hand turning spectral and wan.

The red-orange leaves of fall—gray.

The yellowish moon—gray and gleaming.

The green pine boughs above them—so dark a gray it was black, melding with the darkness of the sky.

"Happy Halloween," Otto whispered.

"And a very happy birthday," Pip replied, voice wavering with a poor attempt at humor.

None of them laughed.

Sixteen

They headed back the way Eleanor and Otto had come, along walking trails that zagged and zigged and climbed and fell. Otto's and Pip's bikes were made for this kind of riding, but Eleanor's wasn't, and the trip to Pip's house had knocked something loose in the front wheel, making it rattle whenever she went downhill and groan whenever she went uphill. Sometimes she had to stop and walk the rickety old thing instead, which slowed all of them down.

"We're close," Otto said at last, as they pedaled along a smooth track between the trees. He'd promised that the place he had in mind would be a good spot to hide, at least while they rested—all of them were exhausted. Eleanor's lungs ached, and she panted for breath, the cold air stinging her throat. Pip seemed like she could keep riding all night. "It's just around—"

"Look out!" Otto yelled, as they rounded a bend in the trees. The dog loomed out of the darkness, its glowing red eyes the only color since the gray seeped in. They clattered to a stop, Eleanor barely jumping free of her bike as it toppled and skidded, coming to a rest in front of the dog. It looked down at the bike and let out a rumbling growl, then shifted its gaze back to them.

Up close, the dog was massive. Bigger than the biggest dog Eleanor had ever seen. Its head was level with her chest, its brow blunt, its fur short and shining. It simply stepped over the bike and paced toward them. They scrambled back, Eleanor grabbing for the fire poker. It caught briefly against the zipper before coming free. She brandished it in front of her.

"Stay back!" she said.

The dog stopped, but it didn't look terribly concerned. Its breath fogged the air.

But it wasn't fog. It was breathing out smoke. Eleanor gulped. "Let us past," she said.

"No," the dog replied in a deep, male voice. Otto squeaked in surprise, and Eleanor realized she hadn't gotten around to explaining about the cat-of-ashes or the whole "talking beasts" thing.

"Iron hurts you," Eleanor said with confidence. The book had told them that much.

Instead of answering, the dog leaped at her. Eleanor yelped and stumbled backward in surprise. She tried to swing the fire poker, but the dog's huge paws hit her in the chest and she flew backward, the poker sailing out of her grip. She hit the ground hard. Her vision filled with sparks, and when it cleared, the dog loomed over her, smoke spilling from between his yellow teeth, his red eyes boring into hers. One huge paw pressed down on her chest, pinning her.

"Little beast," it said in a low rumble of a voice. "You are nothing. You are small. You are afraid."

"Get off of her!" Pip yelled. She had the poker in both hands, and she swung it in a ferocious arc.

It hit the dog and kept on going, swinging straight through him and sending a cloud of black specks and bright sparks into the air. He howled and leaped back, shaking himself and shedding more sparks and ash. A red line glowed across his side where the iron had passed through him. It looked like an ember when you blew on it.

Pip stood with her legs planted and the poker gripped tight. "Field hockey," she said. "Back off, buddy."

The dog let out a snarl. He sank back on his haunches and then twisted, launching himself off between the trees. He knocked against trunks here and there, leaving the bark glowing and smoking, but then he was gone.

Pip stuck out her hand to help Eleanor up.

"Thanks," Eleanor said. "That was really brave."

"That was *amazing*," Otto agreed.

"Don't worry about it. I really wanted to hit something anyway," Pip said, sticking out her tongue. "Now, come on! We should get out of here before it comes back."

They pedaled down the last stretch of the track, which led right past Otto's backyard. The omnipresent gray gave it an ominous look: the swing set loomed, the treehouse crouched among the branches like a hungry beast. There were toys scattered over the lawn, but they were oddly regimented, all lined up to face the same direction. The house itself seemed in a battle between disrepair and the cookie-cutter perfection of the town, everything just a hair off and giving the impression of someone extremely stressed and barely holding it together.

Their vantage point gave them a good view of the road out front and the three cars parked there—a beat-up red Honda in the driveway and two sleek black cars parked on the street. One of them was the car Eleanor had spotted earlier. The black cars definitely didn't match the house with hearts painted on the back door.

"Looks like it was a good idea to get out of the house early," Otto whispered.

Just then, the front door opened. Three figures in crisp black-and-white suits, two men and a woman, marched out to the cars. The woman got into the passenger seat of one of them, the men got into the drivers' seats, and they pulled away.

"Let's not stick around," Pip suggested. Otto led them away, winding through the trees, until they came to an overhang, like a shallow cave. Otto had screened it off with branches and a sign that said OTTO'S PLACE (KEEP OUT! ESPECIALLY EMILY!). Inside he'd stowed a plastic storage box with some comic books and granola bars and a sleeping bag.

"We should be safe here," Otto said. He winced.

"Nowhere is safe," Pip said. "The *colors* are gone—

something's happening all over." She sounded about as freaked out as Eleanor felt. It seemed like things turning gray should be the least of their problems, but instead of getting used to it, she was getting more and more unsettled. Like the whole world had turned dangerous, and set its hungry eyes on them. She shivered, and caught Otto doing the same.

"Does anybody know this place is here?" Eleanor asked.

"Just Emily, and she's off at college," Otto said. "I think we should be okay for a little while, at least."

"The cat-of-ashes said we would be in danger from midnight to midnight," Eleanor said. They gave her blank looks. Right. She still hadn't told them about the cat's visit. She explained as quickly as she could, which still took a while, with both of them interrupting with questions and exclamations.

"So we're in danger until midnight?" Pip said when she was done.

"Do you think we can stay hidden that long?" Eleanor asked.

"I doubt it," Otto replied. "The graveyard dog could track our scent. And the rattlebird can fly. It probably can find us just by flying around."

"So we can't just wait it out," Eleanor said, a little glimmer of hope going dim.

"The book told us how to fight the graveyard dog," Pip said. "The iron worked. There's got to be something else in there, right?"

"I've already looked it over a hundred times," Eleanor said

mournfully. "There are some things about the beasts, but there's nothing about how to beat the curse or the People Who Look Away." Still, she pulled the book out of her bag and opened it to the beginning, letting her gaze wander down the list of titles while Otto shone the phone flashlight for her.

The familiar titles were all there.

But there was another.

"'The Thirteenth Key,'" Eleanor read.

"Well," Otto said, "*that* wasn't there before."

"It's about Jack," Eleanor said, skimming quickly. "And the girl with backward hands, and the hedgewitch. *'The heroes three.'* They go back to the kingdom from the first story, but it's been a hundred and fifty years. Listen. *'The kingdom was as perfect as the day the princess had been taken, not a leaf out of place, not a flower wilted. Yet it was gray—colorless and brittle, full of smiles but without joy. Its people were like marionettes, moving about their lives tugged along by the strings of habit. For the stranger who had blessed and cursed them had crafted from their joy twelve keys. Nearly all their joy had been stolen in this way, but there was a little left, and one key more to make. And should that key be forged, a door would open, and what lay on the other side was more frightening by far than any beast or calamity the world had ever known.'"*

She read on. The three heroes fought their way through the sort of trials that fairy tales often held—riddles and beasts and the like. "*'And then they sought an audience with the*

Storyteller. He permitted them three questions, and each asked one, but none was the right one. They did not know how to close the door for good, but still they had to do something, and so they set out to destroy the keys . . .'"

The heroes succeeded. They broke the keys and kept the door from opening, but it wasn't a happy ending. Some people left the kingdom, and their color returned, and they learned joy again. But more remained, and stayed gray, and the kingdom was perfect and joyless, and the heroes never defeated the People Who Look Away. "*'And they knew,'*" Eleanor finished, "*'that somewhere else, in some other kingdom, a stranger was standing before a king or a queen or an emperor and making them a promise.'*"

"That's an awful story," Pip said. "It's sad."

"They stopped it, though," Otto pointed out.

"And everyone was still miserable. And it didn't stop the bad guys," Pip said. "It's not a proper ending if you don't beat the bad guys."

"Maybe they would have if they'd asked the right questions," Eleanor said.

"Well, what *are* the right questions?" Pip demanded. "And who do we ask? What are we supposed to *do*?"

Eleanor rubbed her eyes. Adrenaline had kept her up, but now her brain felt like it was wrapped in cotton. For a moment, the immensity of everything that was happening rose up over Eleanor like a tidal wave, about to crash down. But she forced herself to take a deep breath. All they needed was a list. A plan.

"First," she started. She paused, thinking. "First, we should get some sleep."

"Sleep?" Pip said. "You think we should sleep at a time like this?"

"Yes," Eleanor said. "I think we need to sleep, if we've got any hope of staying ahead of the January Society and figuring all of this out. So first we rest. Second, we'll go back to Ashford House. The cat-of-ashes said that there was something important there. She said—*everything in this house has a purpose.* And the book and the article, they were both from Andy Ashford. It's the best place to look for more clues. And then—and then we figure out how to make it to midnight." Midnight to midnight, that's what the cat-of-ashes had said. If they could make it that long, they'd be safe.

She hoped.

The rest of the plan—the *how* part of making it that long—would have to wait until they knew more. *Make the rest of the plan,* she added to the end of the list in her head, and felt a little better.

But not much.

Seventeen

When they got to Ashford House, the driveway was empty. A dark car was parked across the street, and a man sat in it—but his head was tilted back, and he didn't move at all while they crouched in the trees, watching. Asleep.

A few lights shone inside on the ground floor, but no one moved in the windows. They sneaked around the back, just in case the man out front woke up, then propped their bikes against the house so they could go through the kitchen door. Eleanor shut the door with a soft click and they moved down the hall in silence, except for the creak of floorboards. It might give them away, but at least they'd hear anyone else coming, too.

"I don't think the January Society is inside," Otto whispered. "If they just set a guard out front, they must not think we'll come back."

"It *does* seem pretty foolhardy of us," Eleanor admitted, hoping that meant it was actually unexpected and clever.

Then she realized that *no one* was there. It was breakfast time, and Jenny and Ben should have been in the kitchen, but even though the lights were on, it was empty. Eleanor felt her heart beat all the way down in her toes. What if they'd gotten hurt? What if they'd gotten taken?

There was a note on the kitchen counter. The writing was sloppy and big.

> *Going to hospital. Everything ok.*
> *BABY TIME*
>
> *—Be*

He'd been in such a hurry he hadn't finished writing his name; it just ended in a flat line with a tiny bump on it. Eleanor let out a relieved breath. They'd probably hurried out without thinking to wake her up. They must have gone before the January Society showed up. Good. They'd be safer at the hospital.

"They should be safe there," Otto said, echoing her thoughts while reading over her shoulder. She nodded, glad he understood what she was thinking. "Where should we start?"

"Back at the clock?" Eleanor suggested.

They trooped upstairs, Pip carrying an armload of snacks she'd liberated from the kitchen.

The clock stood right where they had left it, which Eleanor supposed wasn't so surprising. But something had changed.

The clock's hands now ran the usual way. It displayed the correct time, and the second hand tick-tick-ticked ahead clockwise. As they watched, the minute hand *thunked* forward.

"I never thought a clock working normally would be so spooky," Otto said, and the others made noises of agreement.

Tick tock tick, said the clock.

"What did the cat-of-ashes say, exactly?" Otto asked.

"Something about Bartimaeus Ashford having a huge ego, and hiding things all over. And she said that everything in the house has a purpose," Eleanor said.

"Huh," Otto replied, which was about all that Eleanor had come up with. "Let's look around the house. There has to be something that can help us."

They set to work. They looked in the bedrooms along the hallway one by one, opening every drawer, peering behind doors, even checking behind paintings and mirrors. Drop cloths covered most of the furniture, turning the couches and dressers and chairs into lumpy ghosts, and a thick layer of dust coated everything else. Jenny and Ben couldn't afford the staff to keep the whole huge house clean, so they left most of it closed up. In hibernation.

They found old books and old clothes and a set of lawn darts and an ancient game of Boggle, but nothing that seemed to suit their purpose. They worked their way down to the second floor, where Ben and Jenny's bedroom was, and then to the first floor again. In the great room Otto read the spines of all the books on the shelves. About half of them were Ben and Jenny's. The other half had come with the house and had titles like *A Treatise on the Uses of Deadly Flora in Folk Remedies* and *Practical Mycology* and *Rare Birds and Where to Find Them*.

Pip collapsed onto the big cozy chair by the fireplace and propped her feet up on the ottoman. "This is useless," she said, picking at a loose thread on the arm of the chair. "This place is too big, and we have no idea what we're looking for."

Eleanor had stopped in front of the fireplace. The huge stone fireplace, big enough to walk right into, and the staircase behind it. A staircase that led up to nothing. "Everything in this house has a purpose," she said. "But what's the purpose of a staircase that just leads to a wall?"

She led the way through the empty space where the fire was supposed to be set and up the short flight of gray stone steps. They weren't tall enough to reach the second floor of the house; if they had connected to anything, it would have been halfway between the first floor and the second, but they ended at a blank stone wall instead.

"Is there anything on the other side?" Otto asked, knocking on the stone with his ear against it.

"No. There's a little room on the other side on the ground floor, and one of the second-floor bedrooms above that, and in between there's just a normal amount of wall. There isn't *room* for anything else," Eleanor said.

"But there must be something here. Otherwise it doesn't have a purpose," Otto replied, and began to feel carefully along the wall, stone by stone. "Hold on. What's this?" Otto fitted his fingers under a groove at the edge of a stone and pulled. It swung away on tiny hidden hinges.

The false stone hid a keyhole. It was a big keyhole, five inches tall. You'd need a very, very big key to fit it.

Eleanor bent down and peered through the keyhole. She could see a room on the other side. The light didn't go very far, but she could make out the dark shapes of shelves and other furniture and floorboards that matched the rest of the house.

"That doesn't make sense," she whispered. "There's no room for a room. And that one's huge."

"Normal physics and geometry are just suggestions in Eden Eld," Otto said, sounding pained.

"How do we get in?" Pip asked.

"With a key," Eleanor said. "A very big key." She remembered what she'd thought the first time she saw the clock. The pendulum looked like the end of a fancy key. "I have an idea. Wait here."

ELEANOR OPENED THE glass door and watched the pendulum swing back and forth. She didn't like the idea of stopping it; it made her skin prickle, like the ticking clock was all that was keeping the day moving forward, from midnight to midnight. But she took a deep breath and put out her hand.

The pendulum hit her palm and stopped at once. The clock fell silent. She waited for something horrible to happen, but the house was as quiet as ever. Quieter, without the ticking of the clock.

She wrapped her fingers around the pendulum. She wiggled it. Jiggled it. It moved up and down more than she expected, and carefully she began to shift it back and forth and up and down. The mechanism was definitely attached to something, but it was like it was hooked there, not like it was held there by nails or screws.

Something clicked in the depths of the clock, and the pendulum slid free into her hands. She grinned.

The end of the pendulum had been carved like a key.

The whole thing was about three feet long and made out of some kind of pale wood. The teeth of the key, five of them, were carved with patterns like brambles and flowers, giving them a wild, lacy texture.

Otto and Pip were waiting downstairs, but Eleanor didn't run back just yet. She stood with the key in her hands, balanced across her palms, and savored the moment. She'd figured it out. She was clever, like the cat-of-ashes said. She could beat this. She could win this. She could save them.

The key felt warm in her hands. She wished, more than anything, that her mother was here to see her and know what she'd done. What she'd figured out.

Her smile faltered. She tightened her grip on the key and gave a grim nod.

She didn't need anyone to see her and be proud of her. All that mattered was saving her friends.

She went back downstairs with heavy steps. As she walked toward the living room, she got faster and faster, feeling lighter and lighter. By the time she reached Otto and Pip at the top of the staircase, she was smiling again.

"You got it?" Otto asked.

"I got it," Eleanor replied. She lifted the giant key to the lock. It slid in with a satisfying *click*.

Eighteen

A section of the wall swung inward when they pushed. The room beyond was pitch-black; the light didn't make it up the staircase. Eleanor felt for a light switch. Her fingers closed around a tiny knob on the wall. She tried twisting it, and there was a hum through the room.

The lights came on gradually. They hung in two lines along either wall of the room, with wires strung between them. They buzzed a bit, and they were more yellow than the modern lights she was used to, but they served to illuminate the room.

The color was off. Eleanor blinked, but the view didn't change. Everything outside the room was gray. But inside the room, all the color had returned. Was it protected somehow? This had to be the room the cat-of-ashes wanted her to find.

The room that shouldn't have been there was long and narrow. Deep wooden shelves lined the walls, and glass cases ran down the middle of the room like in a museum. Against the back wall was a long, heavy desk, and beside it was a single window—a circle divided into quarters.

There wasn't a round window on that side of the house. Eleanor was sure of it. And yet, here it was.

They dumped their backpacks next to the door. Eleanor propped the key up next to them and they made their way slowly down the room. Many of the shelves and cases were empty, as if waiting to be filled, but the rest held an assortment of seemingly random objects. A deck of strange cards, a scarab carved out of black stone, a cracked hand mirror, a coin so old it had turned green. She picked up the coin, trying to make out the details on its surface, but it was lumpy and illegible. Without thinking, she slipped it into her pocket and moved on.

Eleanor stopped in front of a shelf that held just one item: a small brass box with eight sides. The lid was propped open. The interior had once been lined with green silk, but it was faded mostly to gray and rather tattered. A piece of crystal nestled in the ruined silk, clear as glass. It was just like the one in the illustration—the one the king's sister used to look at the mysterious man's footprints. Eleanor picked it up gingerly and held it to her eye.

The room looked the same—mostly. But a few of the objects in the room glowed with a faint golden shimmer that wavered around their edges.

"Whoa. Look at this," Otto said. He was standing at the window. Eleanor tucked the crystal in her jeans pocket and walked over.

The view outside the window ought to have been the side of the house. The shed, the scrubby grass, the pines. Instead, an ocean rolled and pitched beyond the glass. It stretched in all directions; not even the smallest shadow of land interrupted the horizon. The moon hung full and heavy, reflecting off the water.

Eleanor reached up and touched the window wonderingly. The image rippled and changed. The ripples steadied into a lush, misty forest—not the one outside, but one far older and far wilder. Something huge and shadowy moved among the trees, a long way off. It stood as tall as the trees themselves, and on its head were huge, branching antlers. It turned toward them, and—

Pip swiped at the glass, and the image rippled away before it could see them. Eleanor cast her a frightened look. "That was probably smart," she said.

"I'm not just good for hitting things," Pip said.

Now the window showed a crossroads, two walking paths intersecting in the middle of a wide, grassy field. A woman walked down one of them, getting closer to them. The darkness made it hard to see, but there was something about the woman's silhouette that seemed familiar.

She reached the crossroads and hesitated, looking to and fro. And then she glanced down the road that led toward them, and Eleanor saw her face. Her dark hair, up in a ponytail. Her sharp nose and big, dark eyes.

"Mom?"

Her mother didn't hear her. She seemed to make a decision and turned toward the road that led away from the window.

"Mom!" Eleanor shouted. "Mom, it's me! Mom!" She pounded on the glass without thinking—and the image rippled, and they were looking out over a mountain slope, tumbling down into darkness. Eleanor pressed a hand against her mouth, stifling a sob.

Pip and Otto looked at her with wide eyes. "That was your mom?"

Eleanor couldn't speak. She could barely nod.

"Your mom that lit the fire," Otto said slowly.

"I think maybe she didn't," Eleanor said. She believed that story less and less. Her mother hadn't been hallucinating the things she saw. That didn't mean she wasn't sick—the way her fear had taken her over *was* an illness, but the things she saw were real. She'd tried, tried so hard, to warn Eleanor about Eden Eld and what was coming. She hadn't wanted Eleanor taken. She couldn't have wanted her dead. "I don't think she meant to leave me at all."

"Of course," Pip said. "Why would your mom be bad, too? My parents are the only actually evil ones. Of course." She turned away, arms crossed, and stomped her way across the room.

"Pip," Eleanor said. Otto put a hand on her arm.

"Don't," he said. "She needs to be mad for a bit. She'll come back."

"You guys have known each other a long time, huh?" Eleanor asked.

"Since we were born. Literally. Our moms were in the same hospital room," Otto said. He bit his lip. "I've been thinking about it all. I was mad at the town at first. I wanted to get away from it. But I don't think that's right. I don't think we should want to run away. Our ancestors—some of them, anyway—made a mistake. No. It wasn't a mistake. *Mistake* makes it sound like it was an accident. They made a *decision*, and it was an evil one. And that's why the town is the way that it is. Dangerous in a way no one will talk about or even see. But we can see it. So maybe that means it's on us to stop it."

Eleanor didn't answer. She was thinking about how hard her mother had worked to try to get her away from Eden Eld. Was that the wrong decision? And if it was, was it wrong only because it hadn't worked? No matter how hard she tried to escape, she couldn't get away from Eden Eld. Had it ever been a possibility? Did her mother's fight matter at all, or was she always going to end up here?

"It shouldn't be our job," Eleanor said. "We're just kids. And we didn't agree to the curse."

"It's our job because we can do something about it, though. And because we're willing to," Otto said. "Otherwise, no one would do it at all."

Pip had picked up a walking stick that had been leaning against the wall and was swinging it like a sword. She thumped it on the ground and turned to them.

"Walking stick," she said. "Like Jack has in the stories. Right? So what have you guys found? Or were you just standing there talking the whole time?" She raised an eyebrow at them. It was the tone of voice she used when she argued with Otto in that "we're friends" way, but it was directed at both of them.

"I found this," Eleanor said, slipping the crystal out of her pocket. "It made some things in the room glow. But I don't know why." They looked expectantly at Otto.

"Um. Let's see," he said, turning slowly and looking a little bit overwhelmed.

"The cards are like the ones the fortune-teller used in 'The Glass-Heart Girl,'" Eleanor said, pointing. She stepped to the next shelf. "Hm. This fur hat might be from 'Tatterskin.' Or . . ."

But Otto was looking down at one of the glass cases. "What about this?" he asked. He pointed at a fancy compass in a silver case. It was the size of a pocket watch, and hung on a chain like one, too. Instead of directions like north and south, the edges of it were painted with vines. At the top of the circle was a delicate blue flower. On the opposite side was a trio of spiky thorns.

"I don't remember that from any of the stories," Eleanor said.

"I like it," Otto said. "Maybe not everything we need is in the stories."

"Maybe," Eleanor said doubtfully. "But I really think you should pick something else."

Otto opened the case and took out the compass without responding. "I don't think it's pointing north," he said. "North should be . . ." He turned around, tapping his forehead, until he faced the wall. "That way. And it's pointing toward the window instead. But then, this room shouldn't be here. And who knows where out *there* is." He waved at the window. "We can't expect this room to obey normal laws of magnetism and direction. I should check downstairs and see if it works normally outside the room."

"I'm going to keep looking in here," Eleanor said. She still wasn't convinced that he should take something that wasn't in one of the stories. She'd find him something else. Something better.

Pip was going through her sword-fighting motions again, so Otto shrugged and trotted down the stairs by himself. Eleanor peered through the crystal. The walking stick was definitely glowing. So was the deck of cards. She wanted to call Otto back and see if the compass was glowing, but he'd seemed a bit annoyed with her for not agreeing with him.

"I'm sorry about what I said," Pip told her, stopping her swinging. She blew a strand of hair out of her face with a puff of breath. "I'm glad your mom's not evil."

"I'm sorry your parents are."

"Yeah. But at least that means I was right," Pip said. "And I do like being right."

Eleanor laughed. "Me too," she confessed.

Outside the room, Otto shouted in fear.

Nineteen

Other voices rose, sharp and angry.

"Mom," Pip whispered. They rushed back to the top of the stairs, trying not to make any noise. Otto had closed the door most of the way when he left, so they could peer through the crack together. All they could see from this angle were feet, and only because the people were standing right in front of the tall fireplace, but that was enough to see what was going on. Ms. Foster's sharp heels stood in front of Otto's scuffed-up, dirty sneakers and a pair of black, polished men's shoes. It looked like the man had Otto by the arms.

"Otto, darling," Ms. Foster said. "We have been looking all over for you. You've had us quite worried. Practically beside ourselves."

"We know what you're doing," Otto said. "We'll stop you."

"Yes," Ms. Foster said, unconcerned. "*We*. Where is my daughter? And the delightful Eleanor Barton?"

"You'll never find them," Otto said.

"We'll see about that," Ms. Foster replied. More footsteps approached. Two more men. "Take him out to the car. And search this house. Top to bottom."

Pip's hands tightened on the walking stick, but Eleanor shook her head. There was no way they could fight a bunch of adults. They'd just get captured themselves.

Pip glared at her, but she knew Pip wasn't really angry at her. She was angry at the men below.

"They're so well hidden, you could look all day and never find them!" Otto yelled as they dragged him off. He was telling them to stay put. And Eleanor didn't see what else they could do.

Ms. Foster stayed behind. She turned in a circle, like she was looking around the room. There were tiny daggers painted on the backs of her high-heeled shoes.

"Unacceptable," she muttered. "Simply unacceptable." She sighed. "It will all work out. You've planned for every eventuality. You have this under control."

Eleanor and Pip exchanged bemused looks. Eleanor supposed that it was a good sign that Ms. Foster had to give herself a pep talk. She just wished the woman didn't sound quite so cheered up by it. Pip gave a shrug as if to say *She's always like this.*

"And of course Claire's daughter would be the one to cause so much trouble," she continued. "Always such a troublemaker herself, sneaking off with that boy of hers. I wonder if the girl shows any . . . Not that it will matter, after tonight."

Eleanor thought she was talking to herself, but then a floorboard creaked, and a new voice spoke. "Why do I get the feeling you're making excuses?" a man asked. A shudder of fear went through Eleanor at the first word. Pip stifled a gasp, and they grabbed each other's hands tight. The man had a strange voice. Like honey and like vinegar. Eleanor couldn't see his feet, or any part of him. "You don't *need* to make excuses, Delilah. They don't matter one bit to me or to my sisters. Either you bring the children to the doorway after dark, or you don't. We will be just fine either way. You, on the other hand . . ." He chuckled. "You know the deal. We'll see you after sunset, at the place it all began."

The floorboards creaked. Ms. Foster let out a sigh. "What a horrible man," she muttered, and then she walked away, too, her heels click-clack-clicking on the floor.

Eleanor eased the door shut.

"What are you doing?" Pip whispered.

"They're going to look all over the house. So we need to hide in here until they're gone," Eleanor said. "Then we'll go after Otto."

"We can't let them take him. Who knows what they'll do

to him?" Pip replied, nearly forgetting to whisper in her agitation. "They don't know we're here. We can sneak up behind them and—"

"And what? Hit them with a stick? *Then* what?" Eleanor demanded. "We can't just charge right in!"

"What if they hurt him? We have to—"

"You heard him. Mr. January. He said that they had to bring us to the door after dark. They don't have any reason to hurt Otto until then."

"So what, we do nothing?"

Eleanor balled her hands into fists. She was right. She knew she was right. But so was Pip. Hunkering down here until dark didn't solve anything. They needed a plan, but she couldn't think of one. There were too many pieces missing. "What would Otto say?" she asked.

"'We need to collect more data,'" Pip said in an exaggerated version of Otto's usual hyper-fast voice.

"I think Otto would be right," Eleanor said. "Charging in isn't the answer, and neither is sitting around doing nothing. There are still things we don't understand. Let's look around in here first. We can't go anywhere else right now, anyway. Not with the Society searching the house."

Pip nodded reluctantly, though her hands were tight around the walking stick, and Eleanor could tell that she was thinking about how it would feel to wallop one of the January Society goons with it.

"This is like a museum," Pip said, speaking each word slowly as she thought it through. "So shouldn't there be some kind of . . . record or something? A list of what's here and what it's for?"

Eleanor perked up. "The desk at the back, maybe?"

Pip held out her hand, and Eleanor took it, not sure which of them needed the contact and reassurance more. Pip pulled them to the back of the room.

The desk looked familiar, and Eleanor stared at it for several seconds before she realized where she'd seen one like it before. "This looks like your mom's desk," she said.

"That's what I was thinking," Pip exclaimed. The legs were carved with the same sort of gnarled tree trunk shape. It wasn't exactly the same—the corners were curved instead of straight, and the wood was a different color—but it might have been made by the same person. "Her desk was made by Bartimaeus Ashford. He made stuff for all of the founding families. People are always bragging about 'having a Bartimaeus.'" She rolled her eyes.

The desktop held only a few objects: a silver letter opener, the handle shaped like an elongated owl; an inkpot; an old-fashioned dip pen; and a single sheet of old, brittle paper, set out as if ready to be written upon.

"There's nothing in the drawers," Pip said as she finished her quick examination of them. "Maybe one of them has a false bottom?"

Eleanor frowned at the paper. It reminded her of the paper in the book of tales—and those pages had been blank, too. Until they weren't. If there was writing hidden on it, was there a way to see it?

She took the crystal lens from her pocket. Things had looked different through it once—maybe they would again. She held it up to her glasses and closed her other eye.

Words spilled over the page, written in an elegant script that she struggled to read. She spoke the words aloud for Pip's benefit.

To Whomever Has Found This Room,

The objects held within this vault are safe, or relatively so, the unnatural powers within them benevolent. If you have found your way here, I assume you are clever enough to learn how to use them without my instructions, and I do not have the patience for explanations in any case.

Use what you can, and take what you must. The People Who Look Away must be stopped. Come and find me if you can.

B. A.

"Bartimaeus Ashford," Eleanor guessed, and then she smacked her hand against her forehead. "B. A. is the person who wrote the book! The book of fairy tales! *He's the one that's helping us!* The plaque by the coffee shop said that nobody ever recorded a date of death for him. And the cat-of-ashes talked about him like he was still alive somehow."

"Then he's *got* to be the Storyteller," Pip said excitedly. "In the book the heroes go and ask him questions, but they don't ask the right ones. If we can find him—"

"And ask the right questions—" Eleanor continued.

"Then we can beat Mr. January once and for all!" Pip finished.

Help. Finally they would have help. They had been on their own this whole time, but here was someone who knew what was going on, who knew about wrong things and magic and Mr. January. Surely Bartimaeus Ashford, if he truly was still alive, would help them. And he had to be better at stopping Mr. January and the Society than three newly minted teenagers.

"So where does a somehow-not-dead-even-though-he's-like-a-hundred-and-thirty-years-old guy go to hide?" Pip asked.

"Well, he's not in the house. He built other places in town, though, right?" Eleanor asked.

"Yeah. A lot of the buildings, actually," Pip said. "I bet he's hiding out in one of them! We can search the town." Outside, footsteps thumped angrily across the floor, and Pip deflated a bit. "After they're gone," she added.

For now, they had to wait.

Twenty

They sat and waited and waited and sat, not daring to so much as whisper. Floorboards creaked and floorboards groaned. Voices muttered here and there through the house. It seemed like you could hear the men in suits no matter where they were. Maybe it was another trick of the room.

Once, footsteps came up right outside the door and shuffled around a bit, but they turned right back around.

Eventually, the front door slammed. Car engines started up outside, then faded. Finally Eleanor felt safe opening the door. They crept down together, cautiously, and stopped to listen. No creaking or groaning or voices, and the house felt empty, like it had when they arrived.

Pip bolted for the hallway.

"Pip!" Eleanor cried in alarm.

"Bathroom!" Pip called over her shoulder, and Eleanor

stifled a relieved laugh, realizing that she had the same urgent need.

A few minutes later they joined up in the front hallway. The sun was coming in through the windows now, but the light was weak and thin. Fall light, filtered through clouds. Eleanor felt strange, like she'd been gone over with a rolling pin. Thinned out. Noises seemed too loud and muffled at the same time, and she found herself looking at the door to the hidden room, wanting to go inside, slam the door shut, and never, ever leave.

She did not trust that urge at all. She'd read too many fairy tales entirely. A feeling like that usually came with a curse at the other end of it, and she was cursed plenty enough already. She resolved not to spend more time than she needed to in that room.

"We have until dark," Eleanor said. "That's what he said."

"That was—it was *him*, wasn't it?" Pip asked, chewing on a strand of her hair nervously. "Mr. January?"

"Yeah. It was him. He didn't seem to like your mom very much."

"That's the only good thing I've heard about him," Pip said. Her voice sounded like a bruise felt when you pressed down on it. "His sisters weren't there. Do you think he's like . . . their leader?"

Eleanor made a face. The fairy tale made it seem that way, but she didn't exactly trust fairy tales to be accurate when it came to how important women were. The book never even gave the girl with backward hands a name, and she was at least as important as Jack. "Maybe it's more like this is his project, and they have their own projects."

"Ashford can tell us more," Pip said confidently.

"We'll find him. Then we'll make a plan," Eleanor said.

"You make the plan. You're good at plans. I'll bring the hittin' stick," Pip said. She had the walking stick in one hand and the poker sticking out of her backpack. Eleanor hoped she wouldn't have to hit anyone or anything. They were just a couple of kids. Any fight they got in, they would probably lose.

"We need better protection," she said.

"We have the stick and the poker," Pip replied.

Eleanor had the book out. She was paging through, looking at "Rattlebird" and "The Graveyard Dog" and "Cat-of-Ashes," but apart from the iron shovel the kids used in "The Graveyard Dog," there wasn't much mention of weapons. The cat-of-ashes and the rattlebird never even fought anyone in their stories.

"There has to be a clue," Eleanor muttered.

"What's that one?" Pip asked, and Eleanor stopped flipping pages.

It was a story called "Iron, Ash, and Salt." Three children fell down a well and found themselves in a gray world filled with strange monsters. They protected themselves with iron, ash, and salt—a refrain it kept repeating.

"*They drove the creatures back with iron! They drove them back with ash! They drove them back with salt!*" Pip read. She had a good reading-aloud voice, Eleanor thought. So you didn't just hear the words, you felt them.

"The iron worked already," Eleanor said.

"Yeah, but . . . most things get hurt when you hit them with fire tools," Pip pointed out.

"It's worth a try. There's salt in the kitchen. And ashes in the drawing room fireplace."

They took down the round container of salt from the kitchen cabinet, then filled a sandwich bag with ashes scooped up from the fireplace. Eleanor washed her hands. Pip just scrubbed hers clean on her jeans.

"So," Pip said. "What's the plan?"

Eleanor took a deep breath and held it. "One, get supplies. We've done that. Two, find Ashford. Three, get Otto free. Four, defeat the January Society and escape the curse."

"It seems like step four is actually a lot of steps," Pip said.

"It's a work in progress," Eleanor said with a grimace. "We'll keep figuring it out as we go."

"If saving Otto's part of it, it's good enough for me," Pip said. The loyal fervor in her voice made Eleanor feel warm.

"All right, then. Ready?" Eleanor asked.

"No," Pip said. "But let's go anyway."

Eleanor opened the back door and stepped out. For a moment she thought she'd been wrong, and the sun wasn't done rising. But it was only that the colors were still all wrong. The whole yard was gray. Dark gray tree trunks, light gray ground, pale gray sky of pockmarked clouds. The shed, which should have been a faded blue, was gray, too.

It was worse, somehow, in the daylight. Stranger, eerier. It made the world seem dead—or halfway to dead, at least.

"Do you think it comes back? Color?" Pip asked.

"After midnight," Eleanor said with confidence. "After today, everything will go back to normal."

Pip shivered. "Let's get moving. All this standing still is making it too easy to think."

THEY RODE THEIR bikes along side streets and back paths again. Eleanor took Otto's bike this time, since it was in better shape than the one she'd gotten from the shed, but her face was still hot and sweaty by the time they reached the official border of Eden Eld.

October 31. Halloween. There should have been kids in costumes, people handing out candy. Eleanor had always loved that her birthday was on Halloween. She loved to celebrate, but hated being the center of attention, and so it was perfect. It was like there was a giant party for her—but no one realized it. She could just watch and enjoy.

But it seemed as if all the joy had gone out of Eden Eld along with the color. The witches and pumpkins in the windows had lost their smiles; they stared with empty eyes and blank expressions. No one wore costumes, and everyone shuffled slowly down the sidewalk, eyes downcast. They didn't just look gray—they were *acting* gray. A man walked past with slow, ponderous steps. The wind snatched the hat from his head and sent it bumping and rolling down the sidewalk. He halted, half turned, and watched it for a moment. Then he just kept moving.

Pip and Eleanor clung together and walked slowly. Any one of these people could be part of the January Society. Any one of them could be dangerous.

A gleaming black car pulled onto the street a few blocks away. It looked just like the ones that had pulled up outside of Otto's house. Pip gripped Eleanor's arm and hissed a wordless warning.

"This way!" Eleanor said, and dragged her into an alleyway beside them. They crouched behind a garbage can as the car whirred past. It was only when it was gone that Eleanor realized they were holding hands again, their fingers laced so tightly together her bones hurt.

She gave Pip's hand one last squeeze before she dropped it, and the two of them straightened up. "Should we—" Pip began.

Clackclackclack! Clackclackclack!

The sound burst in the air around them, and a black shape dropped from the sky with an angry scream, claws raking at Eleanor's face.

Pip let out a yell and swung her walking stick like a bat. The big black bird swooped up out of reach and then dived again. *Clackclackclack! Clackclackclack!*

Now Eleanor could see what was making the sound. It was the rattlebird, and beneath its feathers hung dozens and dozens of bones. Bones of all sizes, rattling at the end of lengths of dirty twine that wrapped him like a net. His claws glinted like steel. His eyes were yellow as a jack-o'-lantern's glow. Pip swung again and missed again.

"Just run!" Eleanor said, and they did, pounding through the alley. They could see the street on the other side.

And then the graveyard dog stepped out in front of them. He put his head down and growled. Eleanor and Pip skidded to a stop.

Eleanor whipped her backpack around and grabbed the sandwich bag that she'd left sticking out of the top of it. She ripped it open and snatched a handful of ashes, flinging them at the dog.

The ashes drifted over the dog's face.

He sneezed.

"I don't think that worked," Pip whispered, as the dog shook his head and growled again.

A low, feminine voice laughed above them. The cat-of-ashes waltzed along the top of the wall to their left. And then, in a single leap, she landed on the ground between them and the dog, swiping at the air in front of his nose and making him jump back.

The rattlebird landed on a dumpster behind them. *Clack-clackclack*. His talons screeched on the metal.

"Language is a funny thing, isn't it?" the cat-of-ashes asked, swishing her tail. "The fierce one had it right."

Ash, Eleanor thought. Ash was the soot at the bottom of a fireplace, but it was also a type of wood. "It's the walking stick," she whispered. The cat-of-ashes purred in approval.

"Told you all I needed was the hittin' stick," Pip said.

"Iron for the dog, ash for the bird," the cat-of-ashes said.

The dog snarled. "Why are you telling them," he said, not bending it at the end of the sentence like a proper question.

"Troublemaker," the rattlebird croaked. "Trickster, traitor, spy."

"Oh, boo. You're just mad your leashes are tighter than mine," she said. "I'm here the same as the both of you, aren't I? As ordered. Now, come on, kids. We're bringing you in. No struggling." She winked one green eye. The creatures still had color, Eleanor realized.

"Tell us what works against you," Eleanor said. "Salt?"

"I'm nice, but I'm not that nice, kid," the cat-of-ashes said. She waggled her haunches and settled into a crouch. "Now, surrender quick before my canine friend gobbles you up and gives your bones to the bird."

"No," Eleanor said. "We're not giving up." She reached over to Pip's backpack and pulled the iron poker free.

"Don't like that one. It tickles," the dog said, tensing up like he was ready to jump. His nose twitched in the air, and he narrowed his eyes at Eleanor. "You have something that doesn't belong to you."

"Now!" Pip yelled. She swung for the bird. Eleanor charged forward, holding the iron poker out like a lance as the dog leaped. Her eyes jammed shut of their own accord and she yanked the poker up in front of her to block him.

Something hot and prickly passed over her skin. She whipped around, opening her eyes. The dog had broken apart in a flurry of sparks and ashes. They swarmed together on the other side of her, forming the rough shape of the dog—but it seethed and billowed like a smoke cloud, not quite turning solid again.

Pip's walking stick swung again and again. She couldn't hit the rattlebird, but she could keep him off.

"Use what you've got, kid!" the cat-of-ashes cried. She reared up on her hind legs. On instinct, Eleanor flung out a hand to block her. The cat's teeth sank into her palm even as Pip's walking stick finally found its mark, and Eleanor screamed in pain.

"Miscreant!" the rattlebird yelled, as his body turned to smoke and ash, still in the shape of a bird. He flapped up high out of reach and hovered overhead.

The dog snuffed and snorted, whirling around like he was chasing his tail. He was getting more solid.

The cat-of-ashes hissed, and her fur puffed up until she

seemed twice her size. Her green eyes were wilder than ever, and between her teeth spat sparks.

Pip had the salt carton out. She twisted it so the holes were open and flung the salt in the cat's direction. It hit her fur and went up in a shower of sparks as she howled and writhed and twisted.

"Ouch! That hurt, you whiskerless wretches!" she yelled as she turned to smoke and ash and streaked away, down low close to the wall. "Curse you all. And good luck!"

Pip and Eleanor charged out of the alley, breaking into the open. Eleanor looked left and right. All she saw was gray. *Use what you've got!* the cat-of-ashes yelled in her mind. The weapons, or—

She yanked the crystal lens out of her pocket and stuck it to her eye.

Color flooded back into the world. Most of the street looked normal, back to red brick and black streets and green trees. She twisted to look behind her. The rattlebird wheeled overhead, gray-gray-gray, and the dog, nearly re-formed, was gray all the way through. The walking stick glowed.

And so did a door, way down the street. It was a huge, ornate door, filling nearly the entire south side of the clock tower wall. Eleanor lowered the crystal for a moment. Without the crystal, the door wasn't there at all. She lifted it and it reappeared.

"I know where Bartimaeus is! Come this way," she said. Pip followed her without hesitation.

Please be unlocked. Please be unlocked. Her breath sliced at her throat, cold and ragged. The dog's snarling and snapping got louder, more *solid*. They reached the door and Eleanor grabbed at the big brass doorknob, twisting desperately.

It opened.

Twenty-One

Eleanor shoved the door open and toppled in without checking what was on the other side. She spun and moved to let Pip in past her, and saw the dog charging up the street, solid again, crossing the distance in only a few giant strides.

She slammed the door shut and threw the lock. The dog struck the other side with a *wham*. The door shook. Eleanor could hear his claws scrabbling, and then a deep howl. It snuffled and snorted at the bottom crack. And then there was only silence.

"I think it's gone," Eleanor whispered. Pip didn't answer. She was looking the other way, her eyes wide. Eleanor turned, too.

They stood in a large room with a vaulted ceiling. The room had all its normal color, but the things in the cases and shelves that filled it didn't. They were gray. A gray sword that looked like it was made of stone. A skeletal gray hand on a gray silk cushion. A gray candle burning with a gray flame.

The shelves had glass fronts and heavy padlocks. The cases were locked up, too, and every item was marked with a number and a date on yellowing paper.

In a glass birdcage, a scraggly, crow-like bird shivered and shook. It thrust its beak against the glass, *rap-rap*, but made no sound.

The only sound in the room was their own breath—and a faint *scritch-scritch-scritch* at the end of the room. A man, white-haired, sat at a big oak desk, nearly identical to the one in the house. The man's head was bent over a big old book, and he was writing something in it with a fancy pen. *Scritch-scritch-scritch. Scritch-scritch-scritch. Scritch—*

He stopped and looked up at them, over the tops of his half-moon glasses. "Well?" he said. "Come on, then. My eyesight isn't what it used to be." He chuckled like it was a joke.

Eleanor bit her lip. Pip lifted a shoulder, like, *What else are we going to do?*

They made their way between the cases. A one-armed doll tracked their progress, her eyes rolling and eyelids fluttering. A book flipped itself open and fanned its pages before slamming silently shut again. When they reached the back of the room, the man set his pen down and sat back in his chair. He wore a vest and tie over a crisp white shirt. He looked the same way: crisp, almost ageless, just a little worn around the edges.

"You're Bartimaeus Ashford, aren't you?" Eleanor asked.

"Miss Barton. Miss Foster," he said. "But young Master Ellis isn't with you, I see."

"How do you know our names?" Pip said suspiciously.

"I make a point of keeping track of these things. And Miss Barton lives in my house, which does make it easier. I must say, you have done much better than most. Though the fact that only two of you have gotten this far does not bode well."

"How are you alive?" Pip asked. "Bartimaeus Ashford would be, like, two hundred years old," Pip said.

"Oh, not quite," he said. "I was nineteen years old in 1851, which gives me a few years yet before my bicentennial, but I will allow that past a certain threshold, a decade does not make much of a difference. What you mean is that I should be dead. And that is so. But you can fool death a little, or at least delay him, by remaining in certain spaces. Certain in-between places. I don't recommend it," he conceded with a small gesture, "but my options are few."

"If you're Bartimaeus Ashford, then this is your fault," Eleanor said, anger rising in her chest. "You're the one that made the deal."

"One of the dealmakers," Bartimaeus said. "I could excuse myself by pleading youth and desperation, but it was an evil deed done for selfish reasons. We wanted to take what wasn't ours and we wanted to keep it, and he offered us that. I regretted it nearly at once, but it took me a shameful number of years to turn that regret into any kind of action. And you are reaping the consequences of my failure. I am very sorry, children, though I imagine that means very little to you."

He uncapped his pen and, muttering to himself, went back

to writing. Eleanor craned her neck. He was recording numbers and dates next to short descriptions of the items in the room.

"What are you doing? Why are you just sitting there?" Eleanor asked. "Why don't you help us?"

"Oh," he said, sounding surprised. "I thought it was obvious. I've already done everything I can. I built the house. I hid my treasures away in it. Things of use I kept there, and I locked up everything of the gray that I could here. I wrote the book so that children like you could learn its warnings. I did my part. The rest, my dear, is very much up to you."

"You're an adult!" Eleanor said, nearly shouting. "You know things! You can do things! You can't just *sit here* and let us die!"

"You won't die," Bartimaeus said. "Oh, no. The People Who Look Away are not killers, Miss Barton. They have never killed a soul—not in Eden Eld, at least, and not that I know of. What good would you be to them dead? Of course, what they mean to do with you isn't more pleasant."

"What *are* they going to do to us?" Pip asked.

"They want to open a door," Bartimaeus said. "The door has been locked for a very long time. Things seep in through the cracks around the edges. I believe you call them *wrong things*. And they are wrong. They're in the wrong world. They belong to the gray world; they shouldn't be here at all. But the man we call Mr. January and his sisters want to open that door. There is something on the other side, you see, or perhaps someone, that they wish to let out. But if they were to manage it, it would have the rather unpleasant side effect of bringing the whole of the gray and the whole of our world into the same spot. Smashed together, mixed together, muddled up like two colors of paint until they're something new. To open the door, they need the keys. And you . . ."

"We're the keys," Eleanor guessed.

"Precisely. Or rather, you're *one* of the keys. You are Mr. January's particular project. His sisters share his ambition, but I get the sense they are somewhat skeptical that this method is the best to achieve it. He can only fashion one key at a time, you see, only with the proper three children and at the proper intervals, but he's quite close. You're the last, in fact."

"And what happens? If our worlds get muddled up like paint?" Eleanor asked.

"I haven't the faintest idea. But do you really want to find out?" Bartimaeus asked. Eleanor shivered.

"Then why would anyone help him? Why would my parents—" Pip bit off the words and looked at the floor.

"We made the bargain expecting we would all be long dead before the true price was paid," Bartimaeus said, with a mild, apologetic tone. "And as time went on, it was the only thing sustaining the town. The cost of change was too high. You must understand, I was very afraid. Afraid of my world. And afraid of theirs. Once we made the deal, he made it clear that anyone who failed to bring him his promised keys would be pulled into the gray world forever. His prisoner. If you make someone afraid enough, they will agree to many evil things."

"I'm terrified," Eleanor said. "And I wouldn't do anything like that. My mom was terrified. She was as scared as anything. And she didn't give me up."

"Your mother was not party to the agreement and not subject to such punishment," Bartimaeus said. "But I take your point. The fear is a reason, but it is not an excuse. They made their choices—everyone in the January Society. Including me."

"So how do we stop it?" Eleanor asked. "How do we save ourselves?"

"I cannot tell you how to save yourselves," Bartimaeus said impatiently. "I am bound by the agreement."

"Like the cat-of-ashes?" Eleanor asked.

"A different bargain, and being a cat, she's found a bit more room to squirm within it, but it's the same concept," Bartimaeus replied. "But," and here he sat back, "if you ask the right questions, you'll have the information you need."

The right questions. Just like in the fairy tale. "We get three?" she asked. Did that count?

He waved a hand. "Literary license. Ask whatever you will. Whether I can answer or not is the limiting factor."

She frowned and looked at Pip. "There must be something more you can just tell us," Pip said.

"There's really very little I can do," Bartimaeus said, starting to sound irritated. "I've spent my resources aiding you as much as I already have. You really must take responsibility at some point."

Eleanor didn't think that was fair. Bartimaeus was the

one—one of the ones—who caused all this trouble. He'd made a mess and was insisting because he'd handed them a raggedy broom and a cracked dustpan that he'd done all he needed to. But she set her jaw. "What is the agreement, exactly?" she said.

"Now that is an *excellent* question," Bartimaeus said. He opened a drawer in the desk and took out a sheet of paper with tattered edges. The paper was thick, and the writing on it was spidery and brown. Signatures, thirteen of them, crowded the bottom. The cursive was hard to read, but she made out a few familiar names. *Barton* was there, along with *Foster* and *Ellis* and *Langston* and *Ashford*. Above the signatures was a block of clearer text.

Every thirteen years, on Halloween night, we shall bring to the gray door three children, and put them through the door. The children must be thirteen years of age, to the day, and they must be born in Eden Eld. When one of us should die, another of our blood shall take our place. We will always be thirteen. We will always keep the pact. And if we should not, we will be claimed, one and all of us, and cast into the gray. If we should keep the pact, our town will flourish, and it shall not fade. No plague will touch it. No fire or flood will ravage it. No violence will fall upon it from outsiders. Harvests will be bountiful and winters mild.

We make this agreement on January the first, in the year 1851, with the ones who look away.

"That's it? That's all?" Eleanor asked. She'd thought it would be more complicated. More precise.

"That's all," Bartimaeus said. He took the page back from her and placed it carefully in the drawer. It clicked shut. He blinked at them. "What are you still doing here? What you need to succeed is there. That was the right question. Well done. You may go."

"What if we stayed?" Pip asked. "They can't get to us here, can they?"

"I don't like children buzzing around when I work. And it isn't healthy for living things to stay in a place like this," Bartimaeus said. "The secret room in the house, either. It has a way of stirring things up in your blood. Things you might not want stirred. It has a way of thinning out all the little tethers that keep you in your world. Especially on a day like this."

As he spoke, he rose from his seat, towering over them. His voice seemed to grow deeper and wider, and listening to it was like tumbling endlessly down a hole. And as deep and as strong as his voice became, his body grew frail, thin—almost transparent at the edges.

And then he collapsed back into his seat. His hands trembled. He adjusted his glasses and shook his head. "No. You cannot stay. Not if you want to live. Truly live. Besides. You have a friend to save. Or are you afraid enough to leave him?"

"I could not be more afraid than I am now," Eleanor said, glaring at him. "And I'm not going to leave him."

"Me neither," Pip said. Her voice wavered, but she sounded sure.

"Then use the back door. Off you scurry," Bartimaeus said, pointing his pen at a shadowed corner of the room. "Don't worry, it will take a little while for the hound to nose you out."

Pip and Eleanor joined hands once again and went to the door. It was smaller, tucked between two towering shelves. A rough black figurine holding what looked like a gourd glared at them with triangular eyes from one of the shelves. Eleanor shuddered and pushed open the door.

It opened with a creak, and they stepped out in a courtyard Eleanor recognized at once. They were on the campus of Eden Eld Academy.

The door began to swing shut behind them, but Bartimaeus called out as it did. "One more thing, Miss Barton. If you should happen to see your father, tell him the answer is *yes*."

Eleanor spun around, her mouth gaping, a hundred questions tangling together in her throat. But the door had vanished.

Twenty-Two

Eleanor groped in her pocket for the crystal and put it up in front of her eye, but though the reddish color of the brick appeared, there was no door.

"I thought you didn't know who your dad was," Pip said.

"I don't," Eleanor said. She stared at the wall as if it would explain things to her. She'd asked her mom who her father was, of course, but she'd never gotten very satisfactory answers. She didn't know what to think about what Bartimaeus had said. Could he just be wrong? And if he wasn't, why did he know her dad?

And what had her mother known, anyway?

"Weird old man," Pip muttered. She kicked the ground. Eleanor forced thoughts of her parents out of her mind. For Otto's sake, she needed to stay focused. "And we're back at school. Yay."

"On a Saturday," Eleanor said. "At least no one's here. But we should find somewhere to hide."

"The library," Pip suggested. "We can hide in the archives. The only person who ever goes in there is Mrs. Zimmerman, and she moved here from Portland four months ago. There's no way she's January Society."

They raided a vending machine along the way—Eleanor could hear Pip's stomach growling—and darted around to avoid being seen from any of the windows. They wedged themselves between two stacks of old newspapers and split up the bags of kale chips and edamame puffs. Eleanor hoped Otto was getting something to eat, and that they were keeping him somewhere comfortable. There was no reason to hurt him, was there? They just didn't want him running away.

"I don't think we're going to be able to find Otto wherever they're keeping him," Eleanor said. "He could be anywhere."

"We can't give up," Pip replied.

"I'm not giving up. We just need to find out where the door is. We know they're bringing him there. We can save him when they do, and then run away and hide."

"They need all three of us for the deal. Maybe it would be better for the two of us to hide and wait it out," Pip said.

"They'll probably put Otto through the door either way, if they think it might save even some of them," Eleanor said.

"Yeah. You're probably right," Pip said. "So then . . . where's the door?"

"I don't know. The Founders' Memorial?" Eleanor guessed.

Pip made a face. "I doubt it. It's in the middle of Main Street Square. There's a Halloween festival there every year." She looked grim. "Do you think . . . do you think that's so that they know everyone will be there and won't accidentally stumble on the Society? So no one interrupts them?"

"Who organizes it?"

"The January Society," Pip said. "They run *everything* in Eden Eld."

"Not after tonight," Eleanor said fiercely, as if by saying it she could make it true. "After tonight, there won't *be* a January Society. Because they'll all be in the gray. And we won't be."

If the door wasn't at the Founders' Memorial, where would it be? Eleanor searched around the room until she found a set of long, flat drawers that were full of maps. They were all sorts of maps, new and old—elevation maps, maps of the county, maps of specific places in Eden Eld. She sifted through them until she found one marked *Eden Eld—1898*. It was in a wide, flat cardboard box with tissue paper over it. She pulled out the box and set it on top of the bureau of drawers, setting the tissue paper aside.

The map was drawn in dark gray ink, or maybe black ink that had faded—or maybe it was some other color entirely, and it was only the gray world making that way. She started to run her finger over the line of the river that snaked along the southern edge of town.

"Don't touch that!" Pip warned her. "You need to wear the

special gloves." She yanked open a small drawer and fetched out a pair of thin white gloves.

Eleanor flushed. She should have known that. She was the one that loved old books and things. She pulled the gloves on and went back to peering at the map.

The streets branched out from Eden Eld, with closer-together streets at the center. It looked like a spiderweb with too many right angles. The streets weren't as dense on the map as they were in modern day, and the town was much smaller, but that meant it was easier to see everything—and she figured wherever the door was, it would be roughly the same now as it was back then.

"I don't see anything obvious," she said.

"They aren't exactly going to write *evil gray door* on a map," Pip pointed out.

"I guess not." Eleanor's hand throbbed. She touched the shiny burned skin and felt the puffy flesh and painful divots where the cat-of-ashes had bitten her. She'd cleaned the bite with wipes from a first aid kit they found in the back of the room, but it still hurt.

What did they know? Her mind was spinning with a dozen things. *Make a list.*

Gray world. Door. Thirteens. Halloween. Iron, ash, and salt. The People Who Look Away. Mr. January. Palindromes.

Palindromes.

She traced a street that ran along the west side of Eden Eld before hooking toward the center of town. "Renner Road," she read.

Pip looked confused. Then her eyes widened. "R-e-n-n-e-r. Forward and back. It's a palindrome."

"Are there any others?" Eleanor asked. They pored over the map together, fingers moving from one spidery line to the next.

"Here!" Pip declared. "Civic Boulevard."

"Look. Level Avenue," Eleanor said. They ran their fingers toward each other, tracing the lines of the roads. Together they formed a triangle—directly around the meadow outside of Eden Eld Academy.

"Here," Pip said. "They're coming here."

Twenty-Three

Time ticked away, the afternoon sliding past them with alarming speed. Eleanor and Pip sat across from each other, backs against the bureaus of maps, their feet meeting in the middle. Eleanor was more tired than she could ever remember being in her life. They had been running and hiding so long and so often that they'd stayed ahead of all her emotions and her confusion and her worries, and all the new information she learned. She'd known they were there, but now they crashed down on her, filling her up until her skin felt tight and hot.

Her mother was out there somewhere, and she hadn't been *well* but she hadn't been *bad,* either. She'd really been protecting Eleanor. Trying to save her from Eden Eld. And the fire—if she hadn't set that, it changed everything.

But she couldn't exactly explain that to the police. Or even to Jenny. No one would believe her. What proof did she have? *Well, you see, officer, a talking cat made a vague comment . . .*

And what if she was wrong? Maybe she only wanted to believe what the cat-of-ashes had hinted at. Maybe she was being foolish, holding out hope.

And anyway, what *had* Bartimaeus meant about her father?

The only thing her mother had ever told her about her father was that he was kind and handsome. He hadn't known about Eleanor, that much she was sure of. He and her mom had been in love, but he'd always known he would have to leave—why, her mom left vague. His job, Eleanor thought, but she couldn't remember if that was something her mother had told her or something she'd made up to fill in the gaps.

He left, and only after did Eleanor's mother find out she was pregnant, and by then she couldn't find him. She wouldn't tell Eleanor his name; she said maybe when Eleanor was older she'd talk about him, but now it hurt too much.

And yet Bartimaeus knew who he was. And her father, it seemed, knew Bartimaeus. So was he involved in all of this somehow? Was he part of the January Society? She didn't think so. She didn't think her mother would talk about him with so much love if he was.

It was a mystery, and not one she thought she would solve today. Bartimaeus had sounded like he was giving her an offhand instruction, not an urgent one. Whatever question her father had asked, it didn't have to do with Mr. January and the gray.

"What are you thinking about?" Pip asked. She had tucked one knee up against her chest.

"My parents," Eleanor said. She shifted a little, making the drawers rattle.

"Me too. My parents, not yours," Pip replied. "I was thinking about what will happen if we win. They'll be gone."

"I'm sorry."

"Me too. I won't really miss my mom. She's . . . No one ever really understands. She has this way of saying things that sound cheerful but they make me feel like I'm some kind of gross bug. Except bugs are actually cool and tragically misunderstood, so something worse than that. Like kale chips." She wrinkled her nose, and Eleanor laughed. "She makes me feel worthless all the time. But I kind of like my dad. Other than the evil thing."

"He's not as bad?"

"She's terrible to him, too. He's mostly just quiet. He really likes books. You'd get along," Pip said. "He translates books for a living. Mostly he stays up in his office and doesn't come out. But he used to let me sit on his lap when he worked, and he has an armchair in the corner just for me, so I can do my homework and stuff in there with him. And sometimes he takes me out on adventures. For days at a time. We just go driving or camping, without Mom. He doesn't say much to me at all, not like her, but when he does it makes me feel . . . better. It helps me not believe what Mom says."

Eleanor didn't know what to say. She'd been the one in need of comfort often enough lately that she didn't think anything she said would help, but still she wished she knew the perfect words. But the only thing that would help would be to make it not true, and she couldn't make that happen. Not for either of them.

"I don't even know where I'll live," Pip said. She squeaked her sneaker toe against the tile, scrubbing at a scuffmark without success. "I don't have any relatives in town. Some distant cousins on the Foster side, but we don't know each other."

"You could live with me. Me and Aunt Jenny and Ben," Eleanor said.

"Really?" Pip asked.

"Of course," Eleanor said. They both knew it didn't work like that, but they smiled at each other anyway, imagining it. "We've definitely got enough room. You could have a bedroom next to mine. Or you could be in the other wing, and we'd have to run across the whole house to visit each other."

"We could find every single secret," Pip said.

"I bet there are all sorts of amazing things we haven't even seen yet," Eleanor agreed. "And the house is so big and lonely. It needs more people."

"Like a hundred more," Pip said. "Your house is *huge*."

"It's *ridiculous*," Eleanor replied.

"It's *absurd*," Pip finished, and they giggled. Then Pip hunched forward. "I wish Otto was here."

"We'll get him back."

"I still wish he was here."

"Me too," Eleanor said. They lapsed into silence. For a long, long time, neither of them could think of anything to say.

"I've been thinking," Pip said at last. "Bartimaeus said that you asked the right question. Or a smart question, or something. About the agreement."

"He did," Eleanor said. "But I don't see how the agreement helps us. Other than knowing that the January Society will get 'cast into the gray' if we win."

"It must," Pip says. "It's got to help us, otherwise he wouldn't have said that."

Bartimaeus didn't seem like a particularly helpful person. He seemed more like the kind of adult who would congratulate you and pat you on the head like you were five, in the hopes that you'd leave him alone. But she thought about the agreement anyway, trying to remember every word of it. "All it said was that they have to put us through the door to the gray, and then the town will flourish, and all the stuff about good harvests and being safe," she said. "Wait. They have to put us through," she said again, drawing out every word.

"You figured something out, didn't you?" Pip said, excited.

"The agreement isn't just about what Mr. January wants. It's like he said when he was talking to your mom. *He'll* be fine either way. It's about what the Society has to do to keep from getting sucked into the gray. They have to *put* us through the door. Which means if *we* put *ourselves* through the door . . ."

"Then they lose," Pip said. "It doesn't work. We don't get sacrificed. Except . . . except we'll be in the gray. That can't be good."

"I don't think it's good," Eleanor said. "But I don't know

what it does mean. Maybe the People Who Look Away will be able to get us there, but maybe not. And it gets us away from the Society."

"I still say we run for it," Pip said. "Grab Otto. Run for the woods."

"They've got to expect we're going to come for him," Eleanor objected. "Thirteen adults and just three of us? You really think we can get away and stay away from them? For however long it takes? Hours?"

Pip hunched in on herself. "I could," she said defiantly. Then, "Maybe."

"The only sure way to keep the Society from putting us through the door is to go through it ourselves. That has to be why Bartimaeus wanted us to look at the agreement."

Pip sighed. "Okay. It's a plan."

"Maybe not a good one," Eleanor admitted.

"Better than no plan," Pip said.

Eleanor nodded vigorously. A plan was *always* better than no plan. "So, one: we wait for the Society to bring Otto. Two: we get him loose. Three: we run *to* the door, and go through before they can force us through."

"They're going to be expecting us," Pip said. "But they're not going to be expecting *that*."

"I hope not," Eleanor said.

Before long, it would be dark. Before long, it would be time.

And they would be ready.

Twenty-Four

Darkness fell, and Pip and Eleanor stole through the school hallways. Their shoes squeaked, and the echoes tumbled back on them like they were a whole army of Pips and Eleanors. It was almost enough to make Eleanor feel brave.

Pip remembered that Ms. West always forgot to lock her classroom, so that was where they went. They crouched low as they entered and waddle-walked across the room, dodging chairs and tables, until they reached the window and peered over the edge. The meadow seethed with low-lying fog. Nine hooded figures stood ankle-deep in it, surrounding a small bonfire. With the loose robes and deep hoods, it was impossible to tell who they might be, but none of them was small enough to be Otto.

Pip nudged Eleanor's shoulder and pointed. Another line of hooded figures emerged from the road that led to Pip's house. Four Society members, with Otto marching between two of them, his hands tied in front of him. They'd put a robe on him, too, and he kept tripping on it where it dragged on the ground.

"Go time," Pip whispered.

"Ready?" Eleanor asked.

Pip tapped the poker and the walking stick, which were hooked to either side of her backpack. "Hittin' sticks engaged. You?"

Eleanor adjusted the wire they'd used to attach the crystal to one eye of her glasses, then checked the baggie of salt she'd tucked into her pocket. "Ready," she said.

"Then we get in, get Otto, and get through the door. Wait for midnight, get back out, don't get eaten by monsters or whatever's on the other side," Pip said.

As plans went, it admittedly needed refinement. Eleanor couldn't help but feel she'd let them down in the tactics department. But it wasn't like they'd had a lot of time. Or resources. Or help.

They skulked back into the hallway and jogged to the nearest set of doors. They'd raided the gym for sweatshirts in Eden Eld blue, which had turned a nice, dark gray without color, helping them blend in with the shadows. Pip pulled her hood up to hide her pale skin and bright hair, which managed to look shiny even with all the color gone.

They stuck close to the building as long as they could. The four figures and Otto had reached the others, with all of the adults forming a wide circle. One held Otto's shoulders, keeping him rooted in front of her—it *was* a her. Eleanor could see the perfect, long fingernails even from here. Ms. Foster.

The murmur of voices was too low for them to hear, but Pip had come prepared. When she'd left her room, she'd shoved some of her spy gear into her bag—including what looked like a cross between a mini satellite dish and a ray gun, with earbuds plugged into it that let you listen in on people from far away. She gave Eleanor one of the earbuds and pointed the dish in the direction of the robed Society members.

The low murmur of voices swelled, ringing with a tinny edge, until they could make out the words.

"What do people feel about moving book club to Thursday next week? I have a scheduling conflict, but I really want to talk about this one," a woman said.

"If it's just going to be you arguing with Ted about the symbolism of the color red . . ." someone said jokingly, and there was a handful of chuckles. Coming through the cheap microphone, they sounded like cackling crows.

"Can we please stay focused?" a third voice said. Eleanor recognized Pip's father's voice from the conversation she'd overheard at the house. "We must not forget that this is a dreadful business. A regrettable one. And one that deserves solemnity."

A few feet shuffled, embarrassment palpable.

"Besides which, I believe our remaining guests are here," Pip's father said, and raised a hand in their direction. The hooded figures turned.

Eleanor and Pip glanced at each other in surprise.

"Now or never!" Pip yelled. She dropped the dish, pulling the earbud out as she dashed forward with the walking stick gripped in one hand. Eleanor charged only a step behind her, letting out what she meant to be a battle cry but came out as a strangled yelp.

Panic welled up in her chest. This wasn't the plan. They were supposed to wait for exactly the right moment. Listen and watch until they saw the door, and then take the Society by surprise—or some level of surprise. They knew the Society would expect them to come, but they didn't plan on being spotted right away.

But now Pip was swinging the walking stick around, clipping ankles and making the Society members yell and jump back. Eleanor hurtled straight for Otto, who stared in gapemouthed surprise for a moment, then threw himself away from Ms. Foster, tearing free of her grasp. Eleanor grabbed his elbow.

No sign of the door. No way to run through it. Their plan was in shambles.

"Run, Pip!" she yelled over her shoulder. "Just run!" Maybe at least Pip could escape. That would be enough to stop the Society—even if it didn't save her and Otto.

One of the hooded figures stepped into her path. A hand grabbed her backpack and yanked her back. She and Otto toppled, their feet tangling up with each other. She scrambled upright.

They were surrounded.

Pip backed up until she was with them, holding the walking stick out, but there was nowhere to run. The hooded figures closed in.

Ms. Foster took off her hood. Through the crystal, her hair was bright red and her eyes bright green, as poisonous and beautiful as ever. Through Eleanor's other eye, the gray hardened all the angles of her face, until she looked sharp enough to cut, and more wicked than ever. "Pip. Dear. This will be easier if you put down the . . . stick."

"It was a trap," Otto said miserably as Eleanor pulled him up to his feet. "They knew you were coming."

"We know they know," Pip said glumly.

"You should have left me," Otto said.

"We couldn't leave you. Even if it was a trap," Eleanor said. "We had a plan. It just . . . didn't work." Her fault. She should have thought it through better. There must have been some angle she didn't consider. Some secret she didn't uncover.

"Friends," Ms. Foster said. "Darkness has fallen. I know that it is traditional to wait for the minutes before midnight, but given this year's antics, perhaps we should get this over with."

"Agreed," Mr. Foster said. And the January Society, as one, lowered their hoods.

"Great-Aunt Prudence?" Otto said, staring at an old woman with a big mole on her chin. "Really?" He sounded more surprised than upset. Maybe they hadn't been that close.

Pip was staring at a man with a short, blunt nose and a

squared-off chin. The top of his head was shiny and bald, with pale hair clinging on down below. Eleanor matched his position to the voice she'd heard—this was Pip's dad, then. Mr. Foster.

"Mr. Wells? *You're* subject three?" Pip asked, and Eleanor blinked. Could she have been wrong? Was Pip's dad standing somewhere else? "But you're my *dentist*." She looked affronted. "If you were just going to sacrifice me, you didn't have to nag me so much about flossing."

"Speak to your elders with respect, Pip," Ms. Foster said.

Pip muttered something under her breath and glared at her mother, but Eleanor was looking around the rest of the circle. "Pip," she whispered. "If that's not your dad, where is he?"

Pip's head whipped around. Her mouth dropped open in surprise. Ms. Foster chuckled. "Harold? You thought Harold was part of the Society? Oh, he attends the *public* meetings. Enjoys the cocktail hours. But he was always too tender-hearted for this kind of business. I knew I would never be able to make him see the necessity of what we do."

"He's not—he doesn't know?" Pip asked.

"No, darling." Ms. Foster's eyes softened, just a touch. "Does that make you feel better? He really does love you, you know. And I might have, too. Only it was better, you see, not to get attached." Her eyes hardened again, and she jerked a hand. "Better tie their hands. There have been enough delays already, and we want them under control when—"

Mr. Wells hissed a warning, and pointed.

A figure stood at the edge of the meadow, mist roiling around his feet. He was facing away from them, but Eleanor's skin crawled with the feeling of being stared at. She shivered and pulled closer to the others.

Clackclackclack. Clackclackclack.

The rattlebird. He circled overhead. He seemed bigger than ever, and when he flapped shadows shredded away from him like feathers falling out. They drifted toward the ground, but vanished before they touched down.

A low, rumbling growl signaled the arrival of the graveyard dog. He stayed back, circling slowly, watching the Society and licking his chops. His nose worked the air, as if he was trying to locate some scent that kept slipping away.

The cat-of-ashes simply trotted between two startled January Society members and sat midway between the ring and the cluster of children, licking her paw. She twitched an ear in Eleanor's direction.

"Thought you were smarter than this, kid. Oh, well."

Through the crystal, the dog and the cat were gray all the way through, but through her other eye Eleanor could see the red glow that appeared every time the cat swiped her tongue over her paw. Her green eyes kept darting from Eleanor's face down toward the ground. No—down toward Eleanor's pocket.

Use what you've got, she'd said in the alley. She'd meant the weapons, right? The salt? Or had she meant something else, too?

"No time to bind them," Mr. Wells said.

The figure wasn't at the edge of the field anymore. He was halfway across, carrying a cane with a silver handle at a jaunty angle. And he wasn't alone. Two women stood farther back, half shrouded in mist. One tall and slender, with hair so pale it gleamed, and the other smaller, sharp-angled, with hair black as ink bound back in a tight bun.

"Everyone stay calm," Ms. Foster said. "As long as we stick to the terms of the agreement, everything will be fine."

"Most of us have been through this before, Delilah," Mr. Wells reminded her. "Though, Edith, it's your first, isn't it?"

Eleanor started. She hadn't recognized the young history teacher in the dark. "I'm just so pleased and honored that you invited me to join," Ms. Edith said breathlessly. Eleanor wanted to kick her in the shins. Maybe she'd manage it, before they put her through the door.

"Come here, children," Ms. Foster said. Otto shrank back. Eleanor, though, took a deep breath and stepped forward, walking slowly and deliberately toward Ms. Foster. She was done being afraid. She'd face this, and she wouldn't flinch away.

As she passed the cat-of-ashes, the cat got to its feet. Eleanor paused, momentarily startled, and the cat rose up on her hind legs, planting both feet on Eleanor's thigh and butting her head against Eleanor's pocket. Automatically, Eleanor scratched the cat behind the ears, and she shut her eyes and rumbled a purr.

"One last chance, little beast. Be sharp," the cat urged her in a tone low as a whisper, and then dropped back to the ground and sauntered away.

Eleanor swallowed. She stepped toward Ms. Foster, slipping her fingers into her pocket as subtly as she could. They bumped against the hard edge of the ancient coin she'd taken from the hidden room, rough with verdigris.

She slid it out and closed her hand around it, then stopped just out of reach of Ms. Foster.

The cat wanted her to remember the coin. But why?

"You don't have to do this," Eleanor said. She felt at the coin in her hand. Had it glowed when she looked at it through the crystal? Had she thought to check? She couldn't remember. She ran her thumb over it, and the graveyard dog froze in his pacing. He stared at her, stiff as a board.

"I know that you think that," Ms. Foster said. "From your perspective, this must all be so awful! But you must understand, you only think that because you're thinking selfishly. This deal keeps our whole town happy and strong. And it keeps all of us safe. There are only three of you as compared the entire town of Eden Eld. It's simple mathematics."

"Three of us every thirteen years," Eleanor corrected her. "And besides, if the town has to sacrifice kids to stay happy, it *shouldn't* be happy."

"Do you know anything about Eden Eld's economy?" Ms. Foster asked.

"The primary industries of Eden Eld are mining and logging," Pip quoted in a high voice, then snorted. "So what?"

"The mines closed sixty years ago. The last time a tree was cut down for anything other than a better view was the 1980s," Ms. Foster said. "Eden Eld has no industries. Money simply arrives. This town *exists* because of this bargain. It would vanish without it."

"Then let it," Eleanor said. She was only half listening. The rest of her attention was on the dog, who was still standing stock-still. She ran her thumb over the coin again, and he twitched and took a jerky step forward. She'd studied the story of the graveyard dog carefully. She could practically recite it by memory. *The children fought the graveyard dog and claimed his treasure trove,* the story said.

Maybe he wanted it back.

"I will not let something that I have invested so much in slip through my fingers," Ms. Foster said.

"Guess you're lucky you never bothered to spend much time on me, then," Pip said.

"This would have been ever so much harder if you'd been a more pleasant child," Ms. Foster said. "Enough of this. Where's—"

She looked toward the meadow and jumped.

The man wasn't standing in the middle of the field anymore. He stood among them, right in the ring of the January Society, and now he was facing them. He held the cane in both hands, out in front of him with the tip planted in the dirt. The women hadn't moved, like this was his show, his deal, and they were just waiting to see how it went.

"What a delightful gathering," he said in a voice was full of laughter. His face was plain—so ordinary that Eleanor would not have been able to describe it if you gave her an hour and all the metaphors and similes in the world. Except for his eyes. His eyes were solid gray, from one edge to the other. Everyone in the circle froze, like they wanted to step back but didn't dare.

She looked at his feet, but they were shrouded in mist. She couldn't see which way his footprints were turned.

"And these are the stars of the evening," he said. He waved a broad hand at Pip and Eleanor and Otto. "I understand you've caused quite the fuss today, friends! I admire that. Pluck, that's what that is."

"Sir," Ms. Foster began. He held up a hand to silence her.

"No, no need to apologize. I don't care how you get them here, so long as you do. Now, I'm forgetting something. What is . . . Ah, yes!" He snapped his fingers. The sound was loud as a firecracker, and more than a few of the robed figures jumped.

In the center of the field, a door had appeared. It was a plain door, hopelessly ordinary. It didn't even have a frame; the hinges attached to the empty air.

"You know the procedure," he said, wagging his fingers in a "shoo" gesture. "Put them through, shut the door, and that's that."

"Let's be done with this, then," said Mr. Wells distastefully.

Ms. Foster lunged for Eleanor and grabbed a fistful of her

sweatshirt. Mr. Wells took her arm on the other side, and they dragged her toward the door. She tried to keep up, but they were walking fast and she stumbled until Mr. Wells shook her. From the yelps behind her, the others were getting the same treatment.

The graveyard dog paced stiffly alongside, watching her with fixed attention.

"They've got this in hand. Musn't interfere at this stage," Mr. January called, but the dog didn't seem to hear. Eleanor gave the coin a squeeze. The dog twitched again and growled. "Come on, boy," Mr. January said with sharp irritation.

They were halfway to the door. "Hey!" Eleanor yelled to the dog. "Want this?" She held up the coin between her thumb and index finger. The dog's head jerked up, his ears pricking and his mouth falling open eagerly. "Go get it!"

She flung the coin over her shoulder into the middle of the line of January Society members.

The dog barreled toward it, hurtling past Mr. Wells and Ms. Foster. They shouted and bailed to either direction, dodging its massive body as it careened into the procession, scattering the others. She saw Pip haul Otto to his feet and sprint toward her.

"Go go go!" Pip yelled. Overhead, the rattlebird shrieked.

Otto started for the trees. "No!" Eleanor called. "The door! Go through the door!"

"We don't know what's through there!" Otto said.

"Better than here!" Pip shot back, and they charged forward

together. They hit the door as the rattlebird screamed and stooped to dive.

"Don't let them—" Mr. January bellowed, but Eleanor turned the knob and wrenched open the door, and then they were tumbling through.

Twenty-Five

Eleanor was drowning in gray. Not mist—mist had texture and movement. This gray was a flat, solid color all the way through. It was more like trying to look through discolored water. Her hand was a dim silhouette when she held it away from her face. But it didn't have resistance like water; she could move normally, though when she tried to take a step, she stumbled. The ground looked no different than the air.

Everything sounded echoey, but the only thing to hear was her. Her breathing, her heartbeat, her footsteps. "Hello?" she called.

Ello ello ello, the gray called back.

"Pip? Otto?"

Pip ip ip

Otto otto oh

And then a new sound: *shush-shush-shush*. Quick footfalls. The cat-of-ashes appeared out of the gray, her green eyes the only bright things in it. "Now that *was* a bit of cleverness," the cat-of-ashes purred, twining around her legs.

"Thanks for the clue. I thought you couldn't help me anymore," Eleanor said.

"Help you?" the cat-of-ashes said, full of innocence. "I don't remember helping you. I remember biting you. And I remember you scratching me in *just* the right spot. Like another lady I know."

"A lady?" Eleanor whispered.

"Don't fret, kid. You'll see her yet. But not tonight," the cat-of-ashes said. "You've gotten free of that dreadful social club, but you're not out of the woods yet. So to speak. Better find your friends. This place isn't healthy for growing girls and boys."

She started to trot away.

"Wait," Eleanor called after her. "Do you—do you know anything about my father? Do you know who he is?"

"Haven't the foggiest," the cat-of-ashes said. "Honestly, I can't tell most of you humans apart." She flicked her tail and bounded off into the gray.

Eleanor pushed away her disappointment. The cat-of-ashes was a cat, after all, and you couldn't expect a cat to be too helpful for too long. "Pip!" she shouted again.

Pip ip ip, her echo said, and then, *nor or or*.

It was Pip's voice, or what was left of it after the gray stole its share. Eleanor headed toward it, calling out Pip's name again. The next time, Pip's voice was stronger. Then stronger again. And then there was Pip, stepping cautiously through the gray.

She saw Eleanor and lunged the last few steps, catching her in a tight hug.

"There you are! I thought I was going to wander here forever," Pip said. Even through the crystal, Pip was gray all the way through. So, Eleanor realized, was she. That couldn't be good.

"We need to find Otto," Eleanor said.

"He was a little behind us when we went through. Maybe that means he's farther away."

"But which way?" Eleanor asked.

"Otto!" Pip hollered, so loud that Eleanor clapped her hands over her ears. Pip's head cocked to the side as she listened. "This way."

"Are you sure? I didn't hear anything."

"I'm sure," Pip said, and forged ahead. Eleanor had to jog to keep up.

Something odd was happening as they walked. The gray was changing—not getting thinner, exactly. Almost the opposite. It was pressing itself into shapes that looked more and more solid. There were gaps in it now, and then patches that Eleanor couldn't see through at all. Her hand plunged through one tall column of gray and vanished entirely. It made a squelching, sucking sound as she pulled her hand out, and when she poked a finger against the thick patch again it had the consistency of cold pudding.

Every few steps, Pip hollered again. Sometimes she adjusted. Most of the time she kept marching ahead. It wasn't until they'd been walking awhile that Eleanor could hear Otto's voice, much thinner and weaker than Pip's.

Finally they saw him. By now the gray had sorted itself into recognizable shapes: trees, vines, nubbly ground. Everything was still exactly the same shade of gray, and the shadows were weak, like the light was coming from every direction at once, which made it hard to see the edges of things. Otto trudged up to them. He'd ditched the robes and was holding the compass he'd taken from the house cupped in both hands.

"There you are," Pip said. She threw her arms around him and held on tight. "You could get lost in your own bedroom, I swear."

"That's just because it's so messy," Otto said.

"That's just because you're always too busy learning things and doing experiments and making things to have time to clean up," Pip said. "My room's messy for no good reason."

"Your room's messy because you pick a new hobby every five days and then forget about it. And because it annoys your mother," Otto said. They broke apart and grinned at each other, and then the grins faded. Pip scuffed her shoe in the dirt.

"Did any of them follow us through?" Eleanor asked.

"Ms. Foster was right behind me," Otto said. "I felt her fingers on the back of my neck." He turned his head. There were three raised lines, but with all of his skin turned to gray it was hard to make them out.

"Shouldn't they have been sucked in anyway? If they broke the agreement?" Pip asked.

Eleanor shook her head. "It isn't midnight yet. They still have time. We need to stay away from them. *And* find a way out of here. I don't want to find out what happens if we're here at the stroke of midnight."

"Do you have any idea how to get out?" Pip asked. "Because I sure don't."

"I might," Otto said. "Look." He held out the compass. When he shifted around to face the same way as the needle, it lined up with the rose. "They didn't take it away from me when they caught me. I don't know if they noticed it."

"Like a wrong thing," Eleanor said.

"Or like the opposite—if they're wrong, maybe this is a right thing," Otto said. "Anyway, when there were a bunch of them around it would spin in circles. But when there was only one, it would point away from them. And when I was alone, it would point kind of toward Ashford House."

"So it's broken," Pip said. "Compasses are always supposed to point north."

"I don't think this one does. I think it points to safety," Otto said. "It's like in 'Jack and the Hungry House.' The girl with backward hands uses the rose to show which ways are dangerous and which ways are safe. The petals mean safety." He pointed to the rose at the top of the circle. "And the thorns are dangerous." He pointed to the cluster of sharp vines at the bottom of the circle.

Eleanor couldn't believe she had missed that. It had been in the story after all. And she'd given Otto such a hard time about the compass. "You were really smart to pick that up," she said. "I'm sorry, I shouldn't have tried to tell you what to do."

"Oh, no, that's excellent," Otto said. "Pip and I are terrible at making decisions. We just bicker. Or neither one of us wants to pick and we don't end up doing anything. You're good at deciding things."

Eleanor felt her cheeks get hot and was glad the gray would hide her blush. "Well, you're really smart. And you know all kinds of things I don't. So I should have listened to you." She turned to Pip. "And Pip, you are so good at *doing* things. I could plan them all day, but you get them done."

"Aw. I wasn't feeling left out, but thanks," Pip said. She stepped forward and pulled them both into a bone-crunching hug. "I'm glad you came back to Eden Eld, Eleanor. And I'm glad that we haven't gotten sick of each other yet, Otto."

"I mean. A little bit sick," Otto said, and she stepped back and socked him in the arm. He grinned at her.

"Use your fancy compass, brainiac," she told him.

He held it up. The compass needle meandered back and forth a moment, rather like a dog testing the wind. Then it snapped to attention, pointing off between the trees. "That way, I guess," he said.

Off they went.

The trees gained texture as they walked, the gray dividing into dark and light, the shadows condensing as the light became less diffuse. At the same time, the three of them were getting flatter, their shadows vanishing. There was no difference at all between what Eleanor saw through the crystal and what she saw without it.

They had better find a way out of here soon.

"Look," said Otto. He pointed among the trees. In a clearing in the woods stood a door. Eleanor whooped and surged forward—then stopped. It wasn't the same door they'd come through. It was carved with intricate pictures: at the top, a crow spread its wings wide, vines trailed down the sides, and human figures, some of them with wings or horns or other strange things, adorned the center. The knob was silver and it seemed to shine with light reflected from somewhere else entirely.

And in the trees around it hung keys. They were long, though not as big as the one from the clock—maybe six inches from end to end. They were white as bone and the ends of each had a number on them—Roman numerals. I and II and III, all the way to X, XI, XII.

Twelve. Twelve keys, because there had been twelve thirteenth years, twelve sets of children put through the door. They were the thirteenth. The last.

Except they wouldn't be the last, not if they got away. There would be more children born on Halloween—born *today*.

Aunt Jenny. She was in the hospital. She was having her baby, and in thirteen years that baby would be turning thirteen, and Mr. January would come for her. Eleanor's throat closed up, thinking about that girl, thinking about Aunt Jenny, who would never even know what had happened to her, and

Uncle Ben, too—would they look for their daughter? Would they have a funeral?

Would they forget?

"We have to find the way back," Pip said, tugging on Eleanor's sleeve.

"No," Eleanor said.

"Well, we can't stay here," Otto pointed out.

"I mean that isn't enough," Eleanor replied. "We can save ourselves, but what if Mr. January tries it again? What about the kids who come after us?"

"Bartimaeus said that we had it right, though," Pip said. Otto gave her a curious look, but she didn't stop to explain. "The words of the bargain were the important thing."

"Bartimaeus wanted us to save ourselves," Eleanor said. "But that's just so that he can pretend he made up for making the bargain in the first place. So he doesn't have to feel guilty. He told us how to get away, not how to *fix* things. He's a coward, and just because he knows a lot about the bargain and Mr. January doesn't mean he knows what's *right*. Thirteen years from now—"

"Thirteen years from now is someone else's problem," Pip said fiercely.

"That's what Bartimaeus and the other founders figured, too. And . . ." Eleanor trailed off, like maybe if she didn't say the next part out loud, it wouldn't be true. But Pip's eyes widened.

"Your aunt."

Eleanor nodded. "If she gives birth today, that means the

baby's like us. She'll be thirteen the next time Mr. January comes."

Otto made a low, horrified sound. Pip blew out a long breath. "Okay. Then we have to stop things. Forever."

"If that's even possible," Otto said.

"The story said it was," Pip replied.

"But Bartimaeus wrote the story. And I don't think he actually knows for sure," Eleanor said.

"We'll try anyway. We won't let anything happen to your cousin," Pip insisted.

Otto chewed on his lip. "In 'The Thirteenth Key,' they at least stopped things from happening *there*, right? They didn't stop Mr. January for good, but they did stop him from messing with the kingdom or taking any more joy. If 'joy' means the kids, then maybe we can stop him the same way."

"They gathered up the keys and destroyed them," Pip said. "Well. Here are the keys." She gestured to the keys hanging from the branches before them.

"Gather them up," Eleanor said firmly. She walked toward the nearest one. It hung on a gray ribbon, twisting slightly as if stirred by a breeze she couldn't feel, turning the XI marked on it to and fro. She reached for it cautiously. As her fingers grew close, the air seemed to shiver, and then to whisper.

Who is she?

Where am I?

What's happening?

Three voices. Two boys and a girl, she thought, though she

couldn't be sure. They were the eleventh—that would mean they disappeared twenty-six years ago. Her mother would have been a kid. Aunt Jenny would have been just a toddler. Did her mother know these children, know their names? Did she wonder where they'd gone?

Did she know?

Eleanor closed her hand around the key. The whispers went silent. She shuddered.

Pip and Otto stood nearby, each holding a key of their own. They all looked at each other with wide eyes. And then, wordlessly, they turned to the rest of the keys.

The older ones were fainter, the words more indistinct. But all of the voices were afraid. The newer ones seemed to be able to sense her—but they didn't respond when she spoke to them.

Solemnly, they gathered the keys. Eleanor had five, Otto four, and Pip, who had climbed into the trees to get the ones that were higher up, had only three. Their whispering was silent now.

"We need to destroy them," Eleanor said, but her voice trembled. It had been easier to think about before she heard the voices trapped within the keys.

"Do we break them? Or make a fire somehow and melt them down, or . . . ?" Pip trailed off.

"I think they'll break more easily than that," Eleanor said. She tucked four of the keys in her pocket and held the fifth, bracing her fingers as if she were snapping a stick in half. She could feel the give in the key. It was like a bone. And bones broke. She applied a bit more pressure—

Suddenly, Pip gasped, and grabbed Eleanor's arm. "Look! There's someone here."

Eleanor's head whipped up, the key dropping to her side. Pip's fingers twitched in the air, but the January Society had taken both the poker and the walking stick from her when they'd grabbed her. They didn't have any weapons at all— except the salt, which she suspected would only be useful against the cat.

Someone was indeed moving between the trees. They stumbled as they walked, propping themselves up on the trees, but they were getting closer and closer. "Be ready to run," Eleanor said—and then the person got close enough, and her whole body tingled with a jolt like she'd been struck by lightning. "Mom?" she whispered.

Claire Barton pulled herself upright. Her hair was a snarl that fell to her shoulders. Her face had withered to sharp, gaunt angles, and her clothes were tattered and hung limp on her frame, but she was alive. She saw Eleanor, and she smiled. "Elle. You're all right."

"Mom!" Eleanor said, and she rushed forward. They fell against each other. Eleanor's mother wrapped her arms around her, and Eleanor rested her head against her mother's chest, fighting back sobs. "I thought you were gone. I thought you were—"

"Hush," her mother said. She stroked Eleanor's hair. "I'm so sorry. The January Society came for you. I tried to stop them, but they took me."

"The fire—"

"It was an accident. I was trying to fight them. I know a few tricks, or I used to, but . . . I'm so sorry, Elle. I never meant to hurt you." Her thin fingers combed through Eleanor's hair, a soothing, gentle motion.

"We have to get out of here," Eleanor said. She pulled away. "Mom, these are my friends."

"You must be Pip and Otto," her mother said, nodding. "The other two. Otto, I have to apologize to you, too. I tried to warn your parents, but I couldn't make them remember. I should have tried harder."

"It's okay," he mumbled.

"But I can start to make it up to you now," Eleanor's mother said. "Give me the keys. I know how to destroy them. Give me the keys, and I can take you home."

"The January Society is still there," Pip warned.

"I can hold them off while you get to safety," Eleanor's mother said gravely.

"No!" Eleanor said. "They'll kill you!"

Eleanor's mother laughed. "No, they won't, or they would have already. Trust me, I'm better protected than the three of you. Besides, with the keys destroyed, they won't have any reason to go after you." She reached out a hand and smiled. "It's okay. I'm here now. You're safe."

Eleanor took her mother's hand. Her mother turned her

hand to look at her palm and tsked at the bloody punctures where the cat-of-ashes had bitten her. "That nasty creature," she said. "I'll make it regret sinking its teeth into you."

"It's not that bad," Eleanor said. "And besides—" She stopped. Nasty creature? But the cat-of-ashes liked her mother. She said her mother scratched her in the perfect spot, just behind her ear. It was why she'd helped. And what had the cat said about her mother? *You'll see her yet. But not tonight.*

"It doesn't matter," her mother said smoothly. "Just give me the keys, and we can go."

Eleanor's stomach twisted. She glanced behind her mother's feet and closed her right eye, peering through the crystal.

Her mother's footprints were pointed the wrong way.

She drew back, clutching the keys against her chest.

"What is it? Elle, come on. We don't have any time to waste," said her mother who was not her mother.

"You aren't her," Eleanor said.

"What are you talking about? I'm your mother. You have no idea what I've been through to get to you," her mother said, sounding irritated.

"Her footprints are wrong," she said out loud to Otto and Pip, who drew up next to her, protective. "She's one of *them.* The People Who Look Away."

Twenty-Six

Eleanor's mother looked shocked. And then she laughed. It was a low, rolling sound. Her image slipped and slid and ran, like raindrops bending the view through a window.

Mr. January produced his cane out of thin air and twirled it. The top of the cane was a two-headed silver dragon, the heads facing in opposite directions. He planted it in the dirt in front of him and leaned forward. "Again you exceed expectations," he said. He sounded different now. Less jovial, more sharp. "Eleanor Barton. Daughter of a hedgewitch and a man who's far too much trouble for his own health. It's going to catch up with him, and it's going to catch up with you as well one of these days. And perhaps that day is today."

"Try anything and I'll—" Pip said, balling up her fists, but he raised a placating hand.

"Now, now. That isn't how this works, young Philippa. I'm not a man of violence, though on occasion my pets fill that role for me. I am a man of agreements and rules, and these rules were set long before you were born. The Society has failed to fulfill their agreement, and they will suffer the consequences. But *their* agreement and *our* rules are different beasts."

As if on cue, his sisters stepped out from among the trees. Still distant, still facing away, but Eleanor could feel them watching.

"The Society needs to have pushed you through the door themselves; I myself don't much care how you get here. However. *However.*" He held up a finger. "We cannot technically stop you from leaving. Not until midnight. So: find your way out, and we'll leave you be."

"Forever?" Eleanor asked.

"Curious creature," one of the sisters whispered, in a voice like dried leaves skittering over concrete.

"Full of questions," said the other, in a voice like branches scraping together in the wind.

Mr. January merely shrugged. "A key's no good if it won't fit the lock, and after tonight you'll be all the wrong shapes. I'm not saying I won't find some other use for you three, but for now—for now, I'd have no reason to trouble you." He drew a pocket watch from his vest pocket and frowned at it. "I would estimate you have . . . a quarter hour."

"But it's only been a few minutes," Otto protested.

"The gray devours all sorts of things. Time being only one of them," Mr. January said. "Children being another." He grinned a wolfish grin. His lips stretched just a little bit too far, and there was something not quite right about his mouth. It seemed to go on too far, too deep.

One of the sisters sighed. "Now he's playing with his food," she whispered. Her head tipped toward her sister, conspiratorial, but they stayed at a distance.

"Such a shame if it all fell apart at the last minute," the other whispered.

"So like him though," the first replied.

"We never thought this would work," the second finished.

Mr. January's smile looked a bit fixed.

Eleanor swallowed. She turned to the others, beckoning them in close so they could whisper to each other. Mr. January waited at a distance with an air of indulgent politeness. "Do you think he's telling the truth?" she asked.

"I don't know. But in fairy tales, that's the way it works. The bad guys have to keep their word," Pip said. Eleanor nodded. It did feel right.

"Tick, tock, children," Mr. January said.

"We still need to destroy the keys," Otto said. "Otherwise, we've only delayed him a little bit, and he'll still come after your cousin and the other kids."

"Even if we destroy the keys, we only slow him down," Eleanor said slowly. "That's what happened in the story. They destroyed the keys, but Mr. January just started over somewhere else. Started over *here*. I have an idea. But I need all of us to agree." Quietly, she explained.

Pip and Otto were quiet. Pip was the first one to speak. "I'm in," she said.

"You're sure?" Eleanor asked. "Because there's no backing out."

"I'm sure," Pip said, and if her voice wavered, her fierce gaze didn't.

"Me too," Otto said. "For the kids after us and everyone else."

"Then give me the keys," Eleanor said. They handed them over silently, and she cupped them in her hands. Twelve keys, and they would make thirteen, and Mr. January would open that door to whatever horror lay on the other side. But maybe not. Maybe they could be strong enough and clever enough and brave enough to stop it for good.

"You're certainly never going to get out if you don't even try," Mr. January said, sounding both delighted and disappointed, as if he'd hoped for more of a show.

Ask the right questions, Eleanor thought. *Maybe we were just asking the wrong person.* Eleanor took a deep breath. "What makes us the right shape?" she asked. "Is it because we're thirteen, or is it because of the bargain?"

"Now that's a clever question," Mr. January said. "Thirteen matters because the bargain makes it matter."

"Then could a new bargain change things? Make the keys something else?"

"Hm. Change entirely, no. Bend a bit, maybe," Mr. January said. "What are you suggesting?"

"We have the keys," Eleanor said. "And if you could just

take them from us, you would have done it by now." His jaw went tight. She thought she must be right. "If we destroy them, you have to start over completely. And it's taken you more than a hundred years to get this far."

"Much more," one of Mr. January's sisters said, and the other one laughed. His jaw got even tighter.

"So what if we made a new bargain?" Eleanor asked. "We give you the keys now. And you give us a year. If we can't find a way to beat you in a year, we'll go through the door willingly. What would that be worth?"

"Willingly?" Mr. January asked. His eyes lit up, like there were candlewicks burning just behind them. "Oh, that would be worth quite a lot. Yes, enough and more than enough." He licked his lips. The tip of his tongue was a deep, bruised purple.

"But if we do beat you, you have to stop. You never get to try to open the door again," Eleanor said. "You have to give your word. You *and* your sisters."

His sisters hissed in displeasure, but he grinned wider. "Ah. But that is another bargain entirely. For my sisters have their own seasons, as this is mine, and their own means of mischief. Bring them into it, and you'll have to contend with them as well, and not only on All Hallows' Eve."

"If we catch you, we get to keep you," one of the sisters said. She turned. Her face was long and thin and hungry.

"And we are very good at hunting," the other sister said, turning as well. Her face was shorter, rounder, blunt and rageful.

Eleanor swallowed. "We understand," she said.

"Then you have a deal," Mr. January said with a twirl of his cane. "I will see you in one year."

"If we don't get them first," one of his sisters hissed.

"And no helping them, just to spoil our fun," the other sister said.

"I would never risk the cause in such a manner. And I'll expect the same from you," he admonished them.

The women laughed, and in unison, they each stepped behind a tree—and vanished. Mr. January gave the children a steady look.

"You may regret opening yourselves up to their predations," he said. "My sisters make me look like quite the tamed tiger, I assure you. But it's too late now. You're up against all of us. But I *do* rather hope you outwit them, and we see each other again next year. Ah, but midnight approaches, and you'll be needing . . ."

He snapped his fingers and pointed behind them.

Eleanor didn't like turning her back on Mr. January, but she forced herself to look. A door had appeared behind them—not the huge, ornate door, but the one they had stumbled through in the field. The door to Eden Eld.

"Now. The keys," Mr. January said, holding out his hand.

Eleanor approached. She laid the keys across his palm, and as they struck his skin, they vanished.

"One year," he reminded them. And he touched a finger to his brow, and stepped back, and back again, and faded as he did, until there was nothing but the gray, the trees, and the distant sound of rattling wings.

A clock began to chime. The clock from the hall in Ashford House.

"Hurry!" Pip yelled, and she ran for the door, Eleanor and Otto right behind her. Pip wrenched it open.

The meadow lay beyond. Just as gray as the woods, but unmistakably the place they had left. The January Society were scattered around, some of them holding themselves gingerly like they'd been hurt, some of them sitting on the ground. Mr. Wells had a big cut on one cheek, and even Ms. Foster looked rumpled and dejected.

The clock kept chiming—and the Academy clock chimed, too, and in the distance the tower clock was counting out the hour as well, the three of them making the air reverberate. *Three. Four. Five.*

"Before it hits twelve!" Eleanor yelled, and they plunged through.

One of the January Society members yelled in alarm and delight as they stumbled out. Eleanor took off running. Otto and Pip ran with her, a half dozen Society members on their tails.

"This is your fault, Philippa Foster!" Ms. Foster yelled. "I had everything perfectly organized! I had spreadsheets! They were *color-coded*! It was going to be perfect until you ruined it!" Her hand snagged Pip's arm and yanked, pulling her around to face her. Mr. Wells caught Otto by the shirt, and

Great-Aunt Prudence caught Eleanor by the wrist, pulling her up short.

Ms. Foster panted. She wavered on her feet, but her grip looked tight as iron. "I am going to shove you through that door myself, young lady," she snarled.

Pip glared up at her defiantly. "No, you aren't. You're out of time," she said.

Eleven. Twelve.

The clock was done ringing.

The door in the middle of the meadow slammed shut.

Somewhere up in the sky, the rattlebird screamed; off in the forest came a baleful howling.

"No," Ms. Foster whispered. "No. Not once in over a hundred years—it won't be my fault, I won't be the one that—"

But whatever else she was going to say, they never heard it. Color rushed back into the world all at once—and the January Society rushed out of it. Between the space of one breath and the next, they turned see-through like tissue paper, and then clear like glass, and then, with no sound but a soft whisper of air, they were gone.

The pressure on Eleanor's wrist vanished, and she rubbed the skin where the woman's hand had gripped. The skin was white in the imprint of long fingers, but the color was already coming back. The pain lingered longer, but that would fade, too, and there'd be no sign left that the Society had been here at all.

Pip was staring at the air where her mother had been a moment before. Then she gave a quick nod, sniffed heavily, wiped her hand across her eyes, and wheeled to face the other two.

"We did it," she said. "We're alive. We survived. We won. Everything else gets to wait until morning."

Eleanor nodded. So did Otto. They took Pip's hands, one on either side of her, and limped their way out of the meadow.

They had won.

Maybe all they'd won was another year—but they'd done it. And Pip was right.

The rest would wait.

THEY DECIDED TO go to Pip's house. They were all exhausted and starving, and more than a little banged up, and it was the closest safe place—safe, now that her mother and the rest of the January Society were gone.

They made their way up the road, past the place where Eleanor and Pip had crouched as the car prowled by. Eleanor couldn't believe that this was only the next night. In the distance, fireworks went off, spattering against the sky. The Halloween celebration in the square, still going.

"If anyone noticed we were gone, we can say we snuck out to see the festival," Otto said.

"No one noticed, Otto," Pip said bitterly. "That's how they've gotten away with this for so long. No one noticed at all."

She shoved her key in the front door and pushed it open angrily.

A man was standing in the hallway, his hair silvery and his nose long and mournful. He was wearing a trench coat, hastily tied shut over pajamas, and he was in the process of putting on his hat, but he seemed to have gotten stuck just shy of actually managing it. He blinked at the three of them.

"Oh," he said. "Hello there. You're out a bit late, aren't you?"

"Dad," Pip said, stepping forward. "What are you doing?"

He lowered his hat. His fingertips mashed the brim, turning it around and around in his hands. "That's a funny thing," he said. "I have been trying to get out the door, but I keep forgetting why I'm doing it. I get my coat and I get my hat, and then I'm hanging them up again with no notion of why I wanted them in the first place. Except that . . . well. Except that I had the sense that I had lost something, and I had to go and find it."

Pip made a soft little sound in the back of her throat. "What did you lose?" she asked.

"I don't know." He frowned down at his hat. "But it was something very, very important. But it's all right. I don't feel as if I've lost something anymore. I feel quite all right now." And then, in complete contradiction of these words, he burst into tears.

"Dad?" Pip said, stepping forward cautiously.

He grabbed her. Eleanor stiffened and lunged, but he only crushed Pip against him in an enveloping hug, kissing the top of her head again and again. His knees shook, and he sank to the floor with her, holding her against him as they both cried.

Eleanor looked away. So did Otto. They stepped outside, back into the brisk night air, and stood looking up at the cloud-strewn sky.

It was a few minutes before Pip stepped out, scrubbing her red-rimmed eyes dry with her palms. "Hey," she said.

"I guess your dad noticed after all," Otto said.

Pip grinned, the fiercest and wildest grin Eleanor had ever seen on her. "I guess so," she said.

Her father poked his head out the front door. His eyes widened when he saw the two of them. "Oh! You're still here," he said. "I'd quite forgotten. Do you need a ride home, kids?"

"That would be great," Otto said with feeling. "All I want to do is sleep in my own bed."

"Me too," Eleanor said, surprised to find that when she thought of the bed in Ashford House she thought of it as *hers*.

"I'll get my keys and my coat, then," Pip's father said. Then he glanced down. "I seem to already have my coat. Keys, though. Back in a jiff." He vanished inside.

"Is he okay? He seems kind of . . . vague," Eleanor said. "Is he still not noticing?"

"No, he's always like that," Pip assured her, laughing. "Everything's okay."

Eleanor's mind supplied a hundred reasons why that wasn't true. Her mother was still missing. Mr. January and the People

Who Look Away would come back. Their plan hadn't been stopped, it had just been delayed. And they still didn't know what happened now that the agreement had been broken. But she nodded. "Everything's okay," she echoed.

"Everything's okay," Otto said as well.

For tonight, let it be true.

Epilogue

The baby sounded a bit like a tree frog, peeping in her bundle of striped blankets. She looked a little like a tree frog, too, but Ben and Jenny didn't seem to be able to tell. To them, she seemed to be the most beautiful creature in the world.

That, Eleanor thought, was exactly the way that it ought to be.

She sat at the kitchen table, doing her history homework while Jenny rocked little Naomi and Ben bustled about making dinner. Stir-fry, for the third time this week; the man lacked variety, but she couldn't deny it was tasty.

Naomi. She'd been born on Saturday morning. Halloween. In thirteen years, she'd be thirteen. Eleanor watched her scrunched-up face twitch and fuss, and she couldn't help the worry that crawled across her skin.

But it would be different for Naomi. No palindrome for

her. She might be marked by her birthday, but she hadn't been picked out to be forgotten. Not noticed. Eleanor was going to look out for her. She was going to stop Mr. January and his strange sisters long before Naomi's thirteenth birthday ever came around.

And she was going to watch the other two children, too. The ones who had been born the same day, in the same hospital. Hannah and Robert—Bob for short, of course. Maybe their parents knew. Maybe, like Otto's, they had chosen the names on the suggestion of a family member. Someone who belonged to the town's social club.

The January Society was still out there, too. Not the thirteen from the meadow—wherever they were, Eleanor didn't think they could cause any trouble just yet. But they couldn't have been the only ones in on the secret. They would need successors. People chosen to take their places in the agreement, if anything happened. And every one of them would know that Eleanor and the others had ruined what they had sacrificed so much for.

Everything wasn't okay. But it would be.

The doorbell rang. Pip and Otto would be arriving for dinner, and then to explore the house. They needed to find every one of Bartimaeus's tricks if they were going to be ready for what came next.

Eleanor stood to get the door, and paused. Through the kitchen window, the orchard was a dark and snarled thing, branches pinning shadows through like nails. But between two gnarled trunks, she could just make out the shape of a man. He was looking away from her, into the orchard.

He raised a hand and waved.

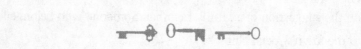

Acknowledgments

This book would not exist without many people, but first among them is Pat Maughan, who gathered us on my apartment floor on the day before Halloween to play a game of children pulled into a world of dark magic and monsters. That game was the seed from which *Thirteens* grew, so first of all: thank you, Pat. And a big thanks as well to the rest of the gaming crew: Mathew Murakami, Michelle Mallett, Andy Smith, member-at-large Thomas Kimmel, and my husband, Mike Marshall.

Secondly, I have to thank the two miscreants who convinced me to take the notes in the back of my notebook and actually write the dang book: Natalie C. Parker and Katherine Arden, thank you for sharing a wild, plane-hopping week with me and inspiring me with your fiction and with your friendship. You are both brilliant. We totally should have gotten those matching tattoos.

And then I have to thank Mike again, for watching our two-year-old during the five intense days of writing the first draft. Also, thanks to the King County court system for supplying the jury summons that forced me to sit in a room with no toddler and nothing to do but write for two days.

Then come those who looked at that lumpy draft and helped shape it into something resembling an actual book. The No Name Writing Group was instrumental, as always, so thank you to Shanna Germain, Erin M. Evans, Susan Morris, Rhiannon Held, Monte Cook, and Corry L. Lee. My agent, Lisa Rodgers, helped me break the book and glue it back together. And my editor, Maggie Rosenthal, had the insights and experience to truly transform the manuscript into something we all adore.

At that point, a whole host of new people got involved to turn *Thirteens* from a manuscript into a real book. I am fortunate to have once again had the masterful Dana Li heading up the cover design, with Sara Kipin's gorgeous illustration bringing Pip, Otto, and Eleanor to life. Thank you also to Kate Renner for the interior design, and to copyeditors Marinda Valenti, Krista Ahlberg, and Vivian Kirklin. And thank you to Kaitlin Kneafsey, my publicist, for all your hard work getting *Thirteens* out to its readers.

Thank you to all of you who helped along the way. And seriously, Pat: this would never have happened without you, and without that game. Happy Halloween, and happy birthday.

**Read on for a preview of
the continuing adventure
with Eleanor, Pip, and Otto in . . .**

They must break the curse . . . before it breaks them.

BRACKENBEAST

The sequel to *Thirteens*

KATE ALICE MARSHALL

Chapter 1

It was raining again. It had rained every day for the last three weeks, and Eleanor was starting to wonder if she should invest in an ark. She clumped along the muddy trail. At least had a good pair of rubber boots, and it wasn't far to Pip's house from school.

She'd had to stay late so she could go to her Yearbook Club meeting. She had to go to her Yearbook Club meeting because normal kids did extracurricular activities, and those extracurricular activities didn't include "searching for Wrong Things" or "researching ways to break curses" or even "cataloging the magical artifacts hidden in a secret room behind the fireplace in your family's spooky old mansion."

When she'd come to Eden Eld, Eleanor had wanted more than anything for people to think she was normal. She didn't want to be known as the girl who saw things that weren't there, or the girl whose mother had burned their house down, or the girl who lived in the creepy old mansion at the edge of town. She just wanted to be Normal Eleanor.

But then she'd met Pip and Otto, and found out that the strange things she saw were real after all. Pip and Otto called them the Wrong Things, and they were all over Eden Eld. The next few days had been a blur of terror and excitement as they discovered that the three of them were at the center of a curse that had been stealing kids for over a century. By the end of it, Eleanor didn't care about being normal quite so much. But she *did* care about Aunt Jenny and Uncle Ben being worried about her. So she went to Yearbook Club and she did her homework and she told them everything was great.

And she *definitely* didn't mention that there was a trio of magical siblings called the People Who Look Away, led by the wicked Mr. January, trying to kidnap her and her friends to use in their evil ritual.

Eleanor and her friends met up after school whenever they could to research more about the Wrong Things and the People Who Look Away, in the hopes of finding something that could save them. Pip and Otto had offered to wait for her to finish with Yearbook Club, but she'd told them to go on ahead without her. She'd meet them at Pip's house.

Which was why she was alone in the rapidly darkening woods when the rain started to glow.

It started as a faint glimmer that Eleanor almost dismissed as a trick of the light, but as the rain got steadier so did the light.

A droplet splashed against the back of her hand and ran shimmering down to the cuff of her jacket.

Her skin prickled. Eden Eld was full of strange things. Most of them wouldn't hurt you, if you stayed away. But some of them were hungry, or angry, or just dangerous the way a cliff is dangerous—it doesn't want you to fall, but that doesn't make landing hurt less.

She picked up her pace. It wasn't far to Pip's house. She could handle a little glowing rain.

Off among the trees, something hooted, a low warning sound. *Just an owl,* she told herself. *It was just an owl.*

But the rattling moan that followed definitely wasn't.

Eleanor started running. Her backpack, stuffed with textbooks, slowed her down and bounced painfully against the small of her back.

The weird light made the air seem to shiver and ripple. She could barely see anything but the streaking colors of the rain—but *something* was moving off in the trees. It was moving with her, keeping perfect pace without making a sound. The glimmering rain dazzled her, making it impossible to see what it was.

She ran faster. So did the shadow. Her breath was sharp and cold in her throat. Her boots slapped against the muddy ground—and then her foot jetted out from under her, hitting a slick of thick mud.

Eleanor hit the ground backpack first and flailed. She flipped herself back over in time to hear bushes shake and snap behind her as whatever was hunting her charged straight for her.

A scream tore from her throat. She ditched her heavy backpack and sprinted away, plunging into the trees. Branches clawed at her face and arms.

Her foot caught against a root. She made a wild grab for the nearest tree trunk and managed to stay upright. She panted, looking desperately around her. The woods were empty. No creature. No shadow-thing. Just the steady plinking of the rain.

"Eleanor!" Pip's voice came from close by.

"Pip! I'm here!" she shouted back. "There's something in the woods!"

Moments later, Pip came tromping toward Eleanor, her walking stick—made of solid ash and excellent for fighting magical beasts—held in a tight grip. The rain had set her red hair into a frantic frizz around her pale, freckled face, but her expression was fierce. Otto, whose tight, dark curls were shimmering with the rain, thrashed his way through the underbrush.

"What's wrong? What's after you?" Pip asked, drawing in close and squinting at the woods. Everything shifted and blurred behind the weird light of the rain.

"I don't know. I saw a shadow. It was big," Eleanor said. "I think."

"Look!" Otto cried out. He pointed as something darted past them, low to the ground. "Is that it?"

"It was bigger than that," Eleanor said, but she couldn't help the uncertainty in her voice. What *had* she seen?

"Whatever this one is, it's glowing," Pip said grimly, pointing the end of her stick in the direction the small shadow had gone. The light seemed brighter up ahead, past a huge pine tree.

Eleanor crept forward behind Pip, who held her walking stick—or hittin' stick, as she liked to call it—at the ready. The light at the base of the tree pulsed like a heartbeat.

"Yahhh!" Pip cried, and leaped around the side of the tree. And stood there, brow creased.

"What is it?" Eleanor asked. She stepped around the tree.

A salamander the size of her foot blinked up at her. Its translucent skin glimmered like the rain, blues and pale purples swirling and rippling. Tiny mushrooms grew around it, and they were glowing, too.

"Don't try anything," Pip warned it. The salamander did not seem inclined to defy her. It stared. After a moment, it blinked again.

"Pip! Eleanor! Check this out! There's more of them!" Otto cried, and burst out from behind a bush, holding another of the glowing salamanders in both hands. Its hind legs dangled. It looked less evil than vaguely confused about its present condition.

Pip gave it a narrow-eyed look and menaced the creature with her walking stick. "Watch out, Otto. It's probably poisonous. Or carnivorous. Or"—she paused, considering—"*scheming.*"

"I don't think so," Otto said with a frown, turning the salamander so he could peer into its face. It stuck out its fat tongue and licked its own eye.

Eleanor sighed and wiped the rain from her glasses with the edge of her sleeve, which only succeeded in smearing it into wet streaks. She must have imagined the thing being giant and frightening because the salamanders definitely weren't either of those things.

Pip lowered the walking stick. "At least put it down until we know what it is," Eleanor pleaded.

"Okay, fine," Otto said with an annoyed huff and set the salamander down. It stayed where he put it but bounced up and down a few times. Otto dropped into a crouch to watch, his tight curls flopping over his face. "So cool," he said.

"Wrong Things aren't cool," Pip said, but Otto just made a shooing motion.

Otto and Pip were best friends. They'd known each other for all of their thirteen years. Eleanor was the newcomer to the group, but she tried not to let that bother her. After all, they shared a unique bond: they'd all been born on Halloween, and they were all descended from the founders of Eden Eld. And that made them cursed.

Last Halloween, the curse had almost taken them. They'd avoided it temporarily, but they knew that they weren't safe for good. Eleanor and her friends had to be on their guard.

"I like them," Otto said. In Pip's opinion, stated loudly and often, he was not sufficiently on his guard at all. "I think I'm going to call them glimmanders. Or glimmermanders. What do you think?"

"I think they're going to try to eat your face," Pip told him, but without much conviction.

Eleanor couldn't see how these placid little creatures could possibly be part of Mr. January and his sisters' schemes. Just to be safe, she took out the flat shard of crystal that hung around her neck on a chain. She'd used it before to see the true nature of the Wrong Things and other hidden magical secrets, and now she lifted it to her eye, peering through it. The salamanders didn't look any different.

"I don't think they're a threat, Pip," she said gently.

"I'm not stupid, I know they're not a threat *this second*. But we don't know anything about them!" Pip glared at her—and then looked down at the ground, taking a deep breath. Eleanor knew she was counting to ten in her head. It was supposed to help her control her anger. Judging by how often Eleanor and Otto found themselves getting glowered at, and how many snapped pencils rattled around in Pip's backpack, it wasn't terribly effective.

"It's my fault. I freaked out over nothing," Eleanor said, trying to smooth things over.

"Yeah, you did," Pip snapped. She stalked away, marching back toward the path.

Otto glanced at Eleanor, wounded worry on his face. Otto had big, dark brown eyes, light brown skin, and a wide, expressive mouth that was quick to smile or frown. That was one of her favorite things about Otto—he never hid what he felt. "Did I say something wrong?" he asked.

"I don't think so," Eleanor replied. "I'm pretty sure she's mad at me. Again." She wasn't like Otto. She thought about every expression, every word, always aware of how she seemed to other people. And right now, she was trying to sound reassuring and confident, even though her stomach was one big knot of anxiety. "It's just hard, you know?"

"No, I don't. And that's the problem, isn't it? I have a totally normal family with awesome parents, so I don't understand what it's like. Right?"

The rain drummed against their shoulders and slicked Eleanor's hair down. She could only shrug helplessly. Pip's mother had been one of the people who tried to give them to Mr. January. That wasn't something you got over in five months. Before that, Eleanor's mother had disappeared—and for months, Eleanor had believed she burned their house down, trapping Eleanor inside and almost killing her. It turned out not to be true, but she was probably the person who most understood what Pip was going through.

She hated this. She hated that Pip was hurting and she hated that it hurt Otto, too. And that she couldn't fix any of it.

Pip, shoulders sagging, was trudging back toward them. "Hey, guys. I'm sorry I got mad."

"That's okay," Eleanor said quickly. "We're all on edge. We don't know when Mr. January's sisters are going to come after us." When they'd escaped Mr. January at Halloween, they'd made a deal with him and his sisters. Each of the People Who Look Away would get one chance to try to claim the three kids. If they succeeded, they would turn Eleanor, Pip, and Otto into a key that would open the door to a world of endless gray. If they failed, though, they had to leave Eden Eld and all its children alone forever.

"Can I take another look at the salamanders? With your crystal?" Pip asked. She reached out a hand.

"Of course." Eleanor lifted the chain over her head and started to hand it over.

"Stop!" Pip yelled—but Pip hadn't said anything. Not that Pip, at least.

Another Pip, identical to the one standing in front of Eleanor, charged through the trees. Eleanor froze. And then she looked down.

The Pip with her hand outstretched was standing on a muddy patch of ground that showed her footprints clearly. Footprints that were pointed the wrong way around.